WEST:

Discovery

For Maryneor
May you discover
beauty in all things—
especially in yourself.
Jeni Roe

The path to discovery
begins with the first step... or
page!

Maggie O'Brien

Books in the WEST series

By

Rolan:O'Brien

WEST: A New Direction (1)

WEST: Discovery (2)

WEST:

Discovery

By

Rolan:O'Brien

WEST: Discovery

Book 2 of the WEST Saga

First Edition:

Copyright 2019 by Margaret O'Brien

Cover Art by Marcellia Bombola

This is a work of fiction. Any references to historical persons, events and/or places are employed fictitiously; any resemblance is purely coincidental.

ISBN: 9781794486669

DEDICATION

When we were young girls, far away, in different parts of the country, a television show premiered. It starred a handsome and talented actor who embodied the characteristics we associated with the Old West. Sixty years into the present, we dedicate this book to him.

Thank you, Robert Fuller, actor and our hero, for years of entertainment and enjoyment.

ACKNOWLEDGEMENTS

Tony Gill, President of the Robert Fuller Fandom

Marcellia Bombola for her extraordinary cover art

Susan Schwartz, nurse/author, for her invaluable assistance

www.susanschwartzauthor.co

The Journal of Jessie Llewellyn

The last two days have been a whirlwind of preparations for our trip east- Vin has been laughing at us at regular intervals, as we each suddenly remembered something we absolutely must have for the trip, then found that we had either already packed it or could always purchase it on the way! We will take the stage to Cheyenne and catch the train there.

Mary is a bit pensive -missing her Coop, who has left to act as scout for the Army until the new recruits arrive, but with the promise of seeing him in St. Joseph to keep her going, she will, I believe, enjoy the journey.

We are hoping to arrive in St. Joseph after about three to five days of travel- we both agreed that stopping overnight at least once or twice would be the best way to both arrive as expeditiously as possible and avoid feeling near dead from the exhaustion of constant train travel! We shall make sure that we share a room and Vin will have his own- propriety must, after all, be observed! I shall miss our rides and the uninterrupted private time that he and I have enjoyed, but, needs must when necessity calls.

I am hoping to get this business of Aunt's estate settled as quickly as possible, given the curtness of my communications with Mr. Jacob Sutcliffe, Aunt Martha's attorney! I have telegraphed ahead, giving him an approximate date for our arrival in hopes that he will have everything in order for me. I have no desire to visit Mama and Papa in Illinois, so the quicker I resolve the legal matters, the sooner we can proceed to Virginia and Mary's business there. We shall leave on the morning stage for Cheyenne tomorrow- I pray we will have a safe and peaceful journey!

MARY

The morning dawned early, or so it seemed. I have always had difficulty going off to sleep the night before traveling. It didn't help that it had been a chilly night and the bed was soft and warm… if we didn't have to leave so early, I would have happily snuggled in deeper.

Missing my Coop, I found my thoughts returning to him often since his departure, but the preparations for this trip helped keep my mind busy and not constantly on him… and that last night we shared… if we had only opened up to each other sooner, he would still be here with me… we'd be married… and he'd be on this journey east with me instead of scouting for the Army. I find myself blushing in anticipation of what more he promises to offer once we are married and must admit how enticing the thought is. As I rose from my bed, I sent out a little prayer for his safety and dressed in my travel clothes.

Taking my suitcases out into the hallway, I could hear Jessie stirring in her room. I paused by her door, "Good morning," I said.

Her reply was something muffled, which I took as an assent.

"I'll see you downstairs," I said.

To my vast surprise, Miss Emma and Vin were already up and had an early breakfast started. "Oh, that smells really good!"

"He," Miss Emma, who owned the boarding house, pointed, "made most of it!"

Vin smiled, saying, "You haven't tasted it yet. Don't get too excited!" Looking around, he asked, "Where's Jessie?"

"I heard her in her room as I passed by. I'm sure she'll be along shortly." With that, I heard the bouncing and thumping of luggage down the steps. "Here she comes!"

Vin ran to grab the bags from her. "Perfect timin' little girl, breakfast is hot out of the pan."

With a raised eyebrow. Jessie took a deep breath, "My, how domestic, Mr. Harper, I never knew you had culinary skills."

I looked away as he pulled her to him and I heard him say next to her ear, "There's a lot you don't know, mi corazon, but I'm willin' to teach you."

Hiding a smile, I did the only thing I could, I drank my coffee as though I'd heard nothing.

We wolfed down breakfast. Now that Vin had demonstrated this new culinary talent, at least as far as breakfast was concerned, we would have to be certain to employ it as often as possible in the future.

We wished Miss Emma and a few of the other residents, who were awake at this hour, goodbye.

"Now you have a safe journey," Miss Emma said, as she saw us on our way. Hugging Jessie and me to her in farewell, she said, "I expect you both back here in a couple months!"

When we arrived at the Raynes Ranch and Relay Station, just before nine in the morning, we were informed by the wife of the owner, Mrs. Lilian Raynes, that her husband, Bill, and his partner, (and cousin to Vin and Coop), Jess Cooper, were in town on business... something to do with assisting the Sheriff. Jess had been made a partner in the Ranch and Relay just several weeks ago as a birthday present from his best friend, Bill (and Lilian).

Lilian invited us to retire to the house to await the arrival of the stagecoach while her son, Skip, stabled our horses. She offered us hot biscuits and coffee. Jessie and I both declined, but Vin accepted with a huge smile. It seemed that, much like my Coop, he also had a hollow leg.

It wasn't a long wait before we heard the arrival of the stage to Cheyenne. We could have caught the train in town and begun our journey from there, but we planned to stable our horses with these fine people while we were away. Heading outside, Vin assisted Skip in changing the horse team.

Jessie and I thanked Lilian for her hospitality. Climbing aboard the stagecoach, we exchanged glances, each excited to get our respective business over and return to this country that we had grown to love and the people in it!

COOP

"You look glum, Coop," said Sgt. Ed Whaley. "Missin' that girl of yours?"

Pushin' the food around on my plate, "Yeah... She's off this mornin'... headin' for Virginia..."

Poppin' me on the back, he said, "Buck up, boy! Ain't like you'll never see her again!"

"I should be travelin' along with her... What if somethin'

happens? What if…."

"She meets another guy?" Whaley said in jest.

I felt my cheeks blaze and my fists clench. "She ain't that type," I heard myself growl.

A couple soldiers sittin' just down the table from us turned to look our way kinda nervous-like.

Ed replied quietly, "Sorry, Coop. Didn't mean no harm! Just tryin' to lighten your mood, is all… Boy, you sure have fallen hard for this girl."

"When those new recruits get here and the Major releases me, I am on my way east, and the first thing I'm gonna do when I find her is marry her."

The Journal of Jessie Llewellyn

We are finally on the train heading East- the stage made excellent time to Cheyenne, and we were able to board the train for points east in the early afternoon. We expect to be in Kearney, Nebraska, in the early evening, where we will overnight and resume our travel eastward tomorrow.

I was most surprised this morning to find that my Vin not only has many manly attributes, but he can also cook quite well! He had breakfast ready for Mary and me when I came down with my luggage and it was delicious. I am eager to learn more of his many talents. I wonder what new revelations I shall experience in the future?

Mary is missing Coop, I know, but this trip is providing a nice distraction from her understandable worry and concern for him. I am trying not to speculate on what awaits me in St. Joseph, but I cannot help but wonder - how substantial is Aunt Martha's estate? It is fruitless to dwell on that- I will know when I know!

Vin doesn't enjoy sitting still and just watching the world go by, so he periodically takes a stroll along the train cars- not my idea of pleasant occupation, as crossing the connections between cars and seeing the rails sliding by so fast beneath my feet unnerves me somewhat! I'm sure that he will tell us if anything interesting is happening in the other cars. I have a feeling that I will be eager to stretch out and sleep, even in a hotel bed, after several more hours on this train.

I know how tired I am, and I believe Mary is exhausted as well. It is somewhat ironic- when I first came into the West, riding and walking tired me considerably, as I had been used to carriages and trains. Now, I find the confinement and sitting for hours at a stretch much more exhausting than a ride into the countryside around Laramie! I do marvel, sometimes, at who I am now versus who I was when I arrived in Laramie - have so many new experiences and challenges changed me, or have they made me become truly myself? Such philosophical musings- perhaps it is just my fatigue, but this journey with Vin and Mary is like returning to visit another version of myself. Perhaps that is why I am not particularly interested in seeing Mama and Papa. To them, I am the disappointing daughter with the odd ideas, permanent spinster aunt to my sisters' children and a minor embarrassment to my parents. I wonder, if I did go to see them, what their reactions would be to this "Jessie" - better not to speculate, I suppose.

This hotel is quite comfortable; Vin has a room just down the hall from Mary and me- unfortunately, proximity does not equal opportunity! We shall go out soon and find a place for a meal- I am hoping that Vin and I can take a stroll afterwards. I don't think Mary will mind, she has a sly smile whenever Vin catches my hand or holds on just a bit longer than necessary when helping me down from stage, buggy, or train. I hope Coop is not delayed in meeting us in St. Joseph- I know she is missing him terribly.

MARY

McKearney, Nebraska

October 15, 1874

My Dearest Coop,

We are on our way East and have stopped overnight. Jessie and Vin have taken this opportunity to take a stroll together to "stretch their legs." Knowing that they could use some time alone, I used the excuse that this would be a good time to correspond with you, as the movement of the train makes it impossible to write legibly!

I know we could take a train all the way through the nights and make our journey shorter, but that would also put the two of us further away, faster... this also gives us a little time to see some of the sights along the way...

Oh, how I miss you, dearest... I long for the sound of your voice and the touch of your hand. Look how I go on... one would think we had been apart months instead of only weeks!

I must get this into the Post if it is to go out tomorrow...

All My Love,

Your Mary

The Journal of Jessie Llewellyn

I asked Vin as we walked slowly through the evening light, "Love, do you think I should visit my parents?"

He looked down at me and said, "Little girl- do you want to?"

His smile, as always, made me feel lit up from within, but I gave his question some thought before answering. "Yes and no," I said, hesitantly.

He laughed and said, "'Fraid that's not helpin', mi corazon! Come on, little girl, talk to me."

He pulled me close as we stopped in a shadow between buildings. I raised my eyes to his, so deep a blue in the shadows, and said, a bit tremulously, "They never really accepted me as who I am, Vin... I always felt that I was a disappointment to them, and I didn't want to be! It was like being in a cage with no way out, until I came West, thanks to my aunt. I'm afraid, I guess, that I'll feel caged again if I see them." I leaned into his shoulder, afraid I should give in to tears, but he gently lifted my chin and looked into my eyes, smiling tenderly.

"Te amo, mi corazon, for who you were, who you are, and who you will become... you said that to me once, and it made me feel like the world was made all new and shining. Just keep rememberin' that and you'll choose right. Whatever you choose, I'm always gonna be with you, little girl."

I pressed close, letting the tears fall on his shirt as he held me comfortingly. To be loved by my Vin gave me such joy that I knew I'd never feel caged again, no matter who or what tried to contain me!

VIN

This little girl can be so dadgum strong in a tough situation, but she's fragile, too, in so many ways. I think she's so worried about her family tryin' to put her back in that "cage" that she don't realize how much she's changed… maybe not really changed, 'cause I think she was pretty danged strong to choose to get away from 'em and strike out on her own! It's that spirit of hers what drew me, like a moth to a flame… Any road, I'm with her and anybody that tries to put her in a cage has me to reckon with! My money's on her, though – she's got enough gumption for somebody three times her size and I can't see even her family havin' their way without a fight.

MARY

By the time Jessie returned to our hotel room I was already in bed, tired out from just this first day of travel.

"Oh, I'm sorry honey, I hope I didn't wake you."

"Not at all, I have only now just slipped in." Appraising her I added, "You look… happy."

When she smiled, she looked so lovely, almost like an angelic being with her hair catching the light and lending a halo effect. "I am happy, Mary. Happier than I can ever remember."

Thinking about my Coop I replied, "I believe I understand. Isn't it wonderful?"

The Journal of Jessie Llewellyn

I am beginning to think that I must be a magnet for trouble! Our second day of travel turned out to be more of an "adventure" than we had anticipated.

We had been on the train for about two hours, and Vin was doing his usual stroll through the cars, when the train abruptly shuddered to a stop! Mary and I looked at one another, alarmed expressions on both our faces, and both of us leaned toward the car window to try to see what had happened. We could see nothing and speculated that there might have been an obstruction on the track or possibly some mechanical problem, but no one appeared to tell the passengers anything. There was a buzz of conversation in the car as we waited for resumed motion or some information about why we had stopped so suddenly. That lasted for almost an hour, then the train resumed motion. All of the passengers around us looked and sounded relieved.

I said to Mary, "Thank goodness! Maybe Vin knows something about this - he's been gone a long time."

I was a bit worried, and I believe Mary shared that feeling as she said, a bit nervously, "I wonder what's keeping him?"

Just then Vin entered the car and walked toward us, a reassuring smile on his face. "Everythin's fine, girls - there was a bit of trouble near the mail car, but it's taken care of." He sat down opposite us and both Mary and I asked what had happened, complaining that no one had told us anything.

"Well," he said, "I was walkin' through the cars and I spotted a couple of fellas I was acquainted with," he frowned a bit and continued, "neither of 'em are what you'd call 'honest citizens' and they were sittin' as close to the door leadin' to the mail car as they could get. I saw the conductor comin' along, so I went over to him and told him that there were a couple of suspicious passengers behind me and he should alert the guards in the mail car."

Mary and I were agog to hear more, so Vin continued, "He asked me to come along with him and we went to the car behind us. The conductor said to a man sittin' there, "Mr. Goodwin, this man has some information you need to know."

The fella he was speakin' to, looked at me and asked, "What is it, mister?"

I didn't know this fella, so I asked, "Why do you need to know?"

Mr. Goodwin pulled a card from his vest pocket and handed it to me - seems he's a Pinkerton agent and on the train as a precaution - there's a big shipment of gold in the mail car and three guards, but Pinkerton's agency was hired to provide more security. Well, I told him about Johnny Gates and Curly Williams, the two fellas I recognized, and filled him in on some of their 'business activities' in the past. Upshot was, he went past 'em and into the mail car, so when they tried to bust in, he and the guards were ready for 'em. They're under arrest and off the train now, so you ladies don't have to worry about anythin' else interruptin' our trip."

Mary and I were aghast- both of us a bit disappointed not to have been closer to the events, but also glad that we weren't!

"One adventure after another," I said, "maybe my wish for such things is drawing much more attention than I intended!"

Mary and Vin both laughed at me, and Mary said, patting my hand, "Honey, since you didn't have any plans to rob the train or to send your Vin to the rescue, chalk it up to life's little surprises! I came out west for some adventure, too, but I don't think either of us get any more than we wish for!"

I looked at her and winked, "I don't know, Mary," I said, "both of us have had much more adventure in some areas than we ever dreamed!" She blushed a bit, and said, "You're right about that, Jessie - isn't it wonderful?" We both giggled, and Vin just looked at us and shook his head. He didn't say it, but his face did, "Women! Never understood 'em, and I never will!"

VIN

That Pinkerton fella, Goodwin, was pretty sharp, I'll grant… he'd been a bit suspicious of me, but when it came time to get ready for those two owl hoots, he asked me to come along. I didn't mind – helpin' out the Pinkertons ain't exactly the usual for me, but I knew Gates and Williams weren't real bright and might start shootin', even with the odds high against 'em. Glad there wasn't a big ruckus, though – I feel responsible for Jessie and Mary and the thought of either one of 'em gettin' hurt ain't one I want to carry around with me. Besides, if anything happened to Mary, my cousin would kill me and not raise an eyebrow! Coop is so smitten, it ain't even funny… can't hardly make fun, though, since I'm in the same case with my little girl. Scares me some, I gotta admit – but everythin' turned out all right and the rest of this trip should be an easy ride – at least I sure hope so!

MARY

Lincoln, Nebraska

October 16, 1874

My Dearest Coop,

You would not believe the excitement we experienced on our train ride today!

About two hours into our travels, Vin was already getting antsy and went for a stroll between cars. Around twenty minutes later, the train stopped for no apparent reason. He was gone for so long Jessie and I began to worry until he returned and related his adventure. (Yes, at least one other name comes to mind who could have had an adventure while traveling on a moving train! And, no, I wouldn't put it past you!) There had been an attempted robbery, but it was foiled because Vin recognized the men who dared the deed! He reported their presence to a Pinkerton agent on board and they stopped the robbery almost before it could begin. Our hero!

Jessie is quite proud of her Vin and with good reason.

We hope to arrive in St. Joseph tomorrow.

I miss you with all my heart,

Your Mary

VIN

Seems kinda strange, bein' here in St. Jo with these two girls…. used to think about saloons and the chance for some "entertainment" when I spent any time in a city. Now, it's more about makin' sure my Jessie and Mary are comfortable and watchin' out for 'em. Never thought I'd enjoy this "shoppin'" thing that gals do, but these two are fun to be around! Even stoppin' and waitin' outside dress shops .n't bad... dang! I must be gettin' "domesticated" like cousin Jess calls it! I can think of a couple o' friends o' mine that'd be laughin' their heads off, watchin' me escort two ladies around town. Too bad, fellas – I got the best so even gettin' laughed at don't matter!

The Journal of Jessie Llewellyn

My dear Vin! He has the patience of the proverbial saint! Squiring us about the town and even waiting ever so patiently while we shopped – I have often thought that I was born under an unlucky star, given how difficult it was for me to feel as if I "belonged" in my own family... but every time I look into those deep blue eyes of his, I know that the reverse is true! We are going out for dinner this evening, Vin's choice of restaurant, which he says is quite famous for its food and service... I shall wear the new dress I bought today... it's just the color of my beloved's eyes.......

MARY

St. Joseph, Missouri

October 17, 1874

My Darling Coop,

Just thought I'd start off a little differently as "variety is the spice of life!"

We have arrived in St. Joseph. Blessedly, there were no further incidents along the way.

I know you have been here many times as it is the Gateway to the West. Of course, I passed through this way on my journey from Virginia, as you well know, but the enormity of the place never ceases to amaze me. So many people and buildings- the hustle and bustle, as they say.

We spent the rest of the afternoon just walking and looking in the stores along the way. Vin, I'm sure was bored, bless his heart, but continued to escort us from one place to another. I must confess to purchasing a new hat, as if I needed another one, but it really is sweet and quite caught my fancy.

Vin treated us to dinner at a most exquisite eatery, the White Horse, not far from our hotel. Have you been there? If not, we really must go when you join us.

Jessie and Vin are taking their usual evening constitutional around this new neighborhood. They have been so very kind, including me, but I know they desire time with each other.

Please know you are missed…

With All My Love,

Your Mary

The Journal of Jessie Llewellyn

I am so glad I had a good night's rest last night - I cannot believe it! Aunt Martha has left me $500,000!

I know I must have seemed incoherent when I told Mr. Sutcliffe that I needed time to come to terms with his overwhelming news, but Vin understood, and said, "Mr. Sutcliffe, Miss Llewellyn wasn't expectin' such a surprise. If you'll give us leave, I think it'll take a little time for her to get used to the idea of bein' a rich woman."

Mr. Sutcliffe, who was much kinder than I expected from his previous communications, smiled and said, "Of course, Mr. Harper. I believe a bit of fresh air and time to reflect is just what Miss Llewellyn needs. I shall be here at her service whenever she is ready to conclude our business."

I think I must have stumbled a bit on the stairs as we left the lawyer's office, because Vin looked concerned and sat me down on a bench in the lobby of the building, saying, "Little girl, are you feelin' all right?"

He looked quite worried, so I assured him I was perfectly fine, and then I said, "On second thought, I do feel a bit dizzy!"

He sat beside me and put his arm around my shoulders, "Take it easy, mi corazon, that was some news! Ain't no wonder you're feelin' a bit kerwallopped!"

I giggled, and said, "Is that one of those new words you were going to teach me?"

He laughed, and kissed me on the cheek, "You could say so, little girl- us Texans have lots of interestin' words for things- you'll have time to learn 'em all!"

Bless my dear Vin! He knew how shaken I was as we left Mr. Sutcliffe's office and suggested we take a walk.

"I guess I am rich," I said, pensively. "I'm not sure I like it very much!"

He laughed, and said, "You've always been rich, little girl, just not in money! You'll get used to it."

"I don't think so," I said, "I don't want it, Vin- that kind of money is a burden and I've just escaped from my 'cage.' I won't go back into one!"

"Whatever you want, mi corazon, I'm with you," he said, "just take all the time you need to choose what's right for you."

We strolled along, my arm in his, until we came to a small shop. In the window was a display of odd trinkets and among them was a ring with the same symbol as my luck piece! I was very surprised to see it, as my pendant was the only piece I had ever seen with that design. Vin agreed when I suggested we go in for a closer look. The shopkeeper told us it was part of an estate and had sat in the window for a long time, as no one seemed interested in it.

As we left, I said to Vin, "I wonder who it belonged to, love. I hope it brought them as much luck as my trinket has brought me."

He grinned, and squeezed my hand, saying, "Brought me luck, too, little girl. That's some powerful symbol!"

We laughed together and proceeded on our way to the hotel. When we arrived, Vin said he had an errand to run and that I needed some time to think about what we learned from Mr. Sutcliffe. He said he'd be back as soon as it was accomplished and gave me a kiss before he left.

VIN

I couldn't believe it! Right there in that shop window was a ring with that symbol …. the half-white, half-black circle that's on my Jessie's luck piece… seems like it was just waitin' for us…I been thinkin' hard about her and me…I ain't got a lot to offer somebody like her and I dunno if just me is enough… but I'm gonna take a chance. Ran into Goodwin and what he had to say, along with seein' that ring… ain't never been too lucky at gamblin' but maybe, just maybe, my luck has turned…

MARY

St. Joseph, Missouri

October 19, 1874

My Sweet Coop,

I have begun to date the outside of the envelopes, so you'll be able to read these in order. Instead of Posting, I am dropping future letters at the Wagon Train office for you in the event we have moved onward in our journey.... They were quite kind as I explained the situation and I was told it would not be a problem as you have been such a valued employee. The gentleman with whom I spoke had all kinds of questions about how we met, when we were going to marry, where we were planning on living and on and on. He was very nice, but it seemed as though he didn't quite believe that you were settling down... I made it understood that you definitely were, and very soon at that!

While Jessie and Vin were at her attorney's office, I visited a local museum. Perhaps tomorrow, I shall go to one of the other wonderful museums they have here. Maybe Jessie and Vin will be able to join me...

You are always on my mind, dearest!

Missing you,

Your Mary

The Journal of Jessie Llewellyn

I was in a brown study, trying to decide what to do about such a huge sum... I truly did not want the burden of so much money. I decided that I would take ten per cent of the estate and have Mr. Sutcliffe set up a trust with the rest, to be held for my nephews until their eighteenth birthdays- that way, Aunt Martha's legacy would benefit the next generation. I was smiling to myself, as I thought about my sisters' reactions, when there was a knock at the hotel room door. I arose and went to the door, saying, "Who is it?"

Vin's beloved voice replied, "Just me, little girl."

I opened the door with alacrity and he came in, looking both pleased and apprehensive. I wondered what had happened and was about to ask when he said, a bit breathlessly, "Got somethin ' to tell and somethin' to ask, little girl."

I looked up and said, "Surely, love, go right ahead…"

He took both my hands in his and said, "I saw that fella from the Pinkerton Agency and he's offered me a job as an agent."

I gasped, and said, "Oh, Vin! Will you take it?"

"I think I will, mi corazon - means I'd be workin' on the side of the law and not havin' to drift from one job to another. It'd give me a chance to settle and...." he hesitated, looking very apprehensive, and then continued, "Means I can do what I've wanted to do for a long time now- ask you to marry me!"

He actually looked scared, my brave Vin - and I felt as if the world was spinning around me! I looked deeply into those tender blue eyes and said, tremulously, "Oh, my love, you don't have to marry me, but I wish you would!"

He folded me in his arms, and I began to cry! Poor Vin - it seems I am always dampening his shirt with my tears. He didn't seem to mind, as his kiss took my breath away. Once I had calmed a bit and we were seated in the room's only chair (with me on his lap!), he reached into his shirt pocket and pulled out a small box.

"I'm not about to let you go runnin' around lookin' available, little girl, so I'll just put this on your left hand right away! I want the fellas to know you're spoken for!" and he took the ring we had seen in the shop from the box and placed it on my left ring finger.

I held my hand up, admiring the perfect fit, and said, "Our luck and our love in one place, my heart, together always!"

"Now, little girl, what say we plan to visit your mama and papa- no cage can hold you now!" he said, looking at me a bit severely.

"Yes, love," I said, giggling a bit, "I want to show you off!"

He laughed so hard I nearly fell off his lap! I cannot wait to tell Mary my "news" - I doubt it will be a surprise to her, but I am so full of joy it must be shared!

MARY

St. Joseph, Missouri

October 20, 1874

My Dearest Love,

I have such happy news to impart! I just wish you were here, so I could tell you in person. Are you sitting down? Last night, Vin asked Jessie to marry him! Oh, this is so exciting!

When Jessie told me, she could hardly contain herself! I am so happy and pleased for them and now, she and I will *really* be family!

As you know, I have considered her as close as a sister for a while, but now it will be official!

It is also very romantic how the ring was chosen. You have seen the talisman Jessie wears around her neck? The ring is of the same design! Can you imagine that? What are the chances? It holds such meaning for the both of them.…

Oh, darling, I wish you were here to celebrate the occasion with us!

As always,

Forever Yours,

Mary

The Journal of Jessie Llewellyn

Mary was almost as excited by my engagement as I was- when I told her about it last night she said, "Now we really are family!"

I have never felt so warmed and loved- by both my "sister by choice" and my affianced husband! Vin and I went for a drive this morning outside the city and into the countryside.

I have become so used to the "wide open spaces" of Wyoming, that I was beginning to feel stifled in the city, and I know that Vin feels the same way. It was wonderful to escape the noise and bustle for a while.... I told Vin about my decision regarding Aunt Martha's estate (I was too ecstatic at our engagement last night to even remember what I had decided!).

He understood, and said, "Little girl, you're right- money like that is a burden. I've seen too many men kill for money alone. I've learned that the wish for more than enough to get along on can be a bigger trap than bein' poor!"

I leaned against his shoulder and asked, "So, will you come with me to Mr. Sutcliffe's office tomorrow, so I can settle it with him?"

"You bet, mi corazon!" he replied, grinning, "I wanna see his face when you tell him you don't like bein' rich!"

I giggled, I couldn't help it, as I imagined the lawyer's reaction! "Well, my heart," I said, "just make sure you won't regret marrying me when I'm just reasonably well off!"

"Well, I might," he said, with a smile, "regret marryin' you, I mean, someday, but if I do it won't be because o' that."

I sat up, turned to look him in the eye, and said, in my "schoolmarm" tones, "Just what would make you regret marrying me, Mr. Vin Harper?"

"Whoa, there, little girl" he said, cupping my face in those gentle hands, "I didn't say I would, just that I might! The only way that could happen would be if I got myself killed and left you alone- I'm thinkin' of doin' a dangerous job, mi corazon, and I don't want you to regret marryin' me either!"

I pulled him to me and kissed him with every bit of the love I felt for this man, and said, "Dear love- I know about danger and mortality, and the fear of losing one you love, but for whatever time each of us has in this life, I want it to be spent with each other! Life's a gift, dearest, and I refuse to waste it dreading tomorrow- you are who I want and always will, whatever you do and wherever you go. That is enough to 'get along' on!"

He wrapped his arms about me, and we just sat there, being together in the soft sounds of the countryside- each of us knowing that this was exactly where we wished to be- now and for always.

It has been such a lovely day- I rather hate to see it end, but I must go to Mr. Sutcliffe tomorrow and tell him my decision- I hope he won't become difficult and that Vin can restrain himself if he is! I doubt that Vin would shoot the man, but he might well laugh himself sick at the expression on the face of a lawyer whose very wealthy client tells him she doesn't want to be rich!

MARY

I treated myself to luncheon at a small cafe near the hotel. It gave me the opportunity to ponder all the changes in my life… and Jessie's.

Jessie is a rich woman! She and Vin had been so excited last night when they told me of their engagement that they forgot to mention her inheritance! I hope she is making the right decision in what she is planning... but it is her money and her decision and Vin is behind her one hundred per cent, as am I.

Watching the various couples sitting and chatting together in the cafe or strolling past the windows hand in hand, I could not help but think of my Coop… we'll be together someday soon, I hope...

The Journal of Jessie Llewellyn

I am so proud of my Vin! He didn't burst into laughter at the lawyer's office when I told Mr. Sutcliffe what I planned to do with my inheritance. The expression on the man's face when I told him that I'd prefer not to be rich was priceless! One would have thought that he was being slowly devoured by wolves, so horrified was the look on his face! He did manage to accept, finally, that I meant to do what I said, no matter how much he tried to talk me out of it and told us that it would take at least a week to set up the trusts and liquidate Aunt Martha's assets. Her house would be put up for sale, and when it was sold, the proceeds would be added to the other assets- he promised to draw up the papers needed to set up the transference of her funds to me as well as the trust for the boys. I was also told that I should remain in St. Joseph, as he would need my signature several times as the various legal actions were taken.

I knew enough about the law to ask if I could just give him a power of attorney, but he refused, being unwilling to accept the responsibility for what was now my estate without my being close by. I understood and appreciated his rectitude- it gave me some needed trust in him. Vin nodded at me with approval when I told Mr. Sutcliffe of our engagement and our wish to visit my parents- I think he thought I might back out, even though I did want to show him off!

Mr. Sutcliffe promised to set up a drawing account for me at a bank in St. Joseph, so I would have access to sufficient money to meet my expenses. I was most appreciative, as I was very low on funds.

When we left, he shook hands with me and with Vin, saying, "Mr. Harper, my congratulations on your engagement; Miss Llewellyn, I wish you joy in your future!" He meant it, but he still looked somewhat pained that my "future" would not include a half million dollars!

Vin and I started laughing so hard halfway down the stairs from his office that both of us needed to sit down on the bench in the lobby until we were sober enough to be seen on the street!

VIN

That lawyer fella was just about floored when Jessie told him what she wanted to do about her auntie's money – it took a lot of will power not to start laughin' like one o' them hyenas! We'll be goin' to Jessie's family, once all the legal business is settled. I'm hopin' that Coop will get here afore we leave – Mary surely does miss him. I'd kinda like to brag a little about my girl agreein' to marry me, too! I know that Mary must've written him about it, but it ain't quite the same. Mr. Sutcliffe said he'd set up an account here in St. Jo for Jessie to draw on and that pleased her a lot.... she's bound and determined to pay Mary back for the lawyer fee back in Laramie when it was lookin' like I'd go to trial for the murder of Jessie's bastard of a cousin, Colby Ferris. I'd rather it was me payin', but until I start workin' for Pinkerton, I only got the little I earned from workin' the wagon train.

Ain't spent much, which is a good thing, else I couldn't have afforded to buy my girl a ring! Every time I see it on her finger I almost gotta pinch myself.... only thing that worries me is leavin' her alone if somethin' happens to me...but she's right – we gotta take the chance and enjoy bein' together.......

The Journal of Jessie Llewellyn

When I told Mary about our visit with Mr. Sutcliffe, she laughed almost as much as Vin and I had! I promised her that, as soon as the bank account became available, I would reimburse her for the legal fees back in Laramie.

Her response was, "Take your time, Jessie- I may have to hit you up for a loan one day!"

We laughed, and I was again struck by how lucky I am to have found a "sister" who not only cares about me but is willing to step up when I need help! She was pleased that Vin and I would be going to my hometown of Alton, Illinois, to visit my parents when all the legal matters here are settled.

I said, "Mary, please come with us! I still have some misgivings about seeing Mama and Papa, even though I no longer feel that their 'disappointment' in me matters very much. We can leave word for your Coop where we are going if he has not returned by the time we are ready to leave."

She looked a bit bemused (I am sure she was concerned about Coop and longing for their reunion) but agreed to come. I breathed a sigh of relief. I know I am foolish to have such apprehension still, but Mary and Vin are not only dear to me, they represent how much I have changed and grown since I moved West. I know I will never feel "at home" with Mama and Papa again - my "home" is now wherever my Vin is - but even a freed bird dreads the cage!

MARY

St. Joseph, Missouri

October 21,1874

My Darling Coop,

Again, you will not believe the news! Jessie has come into quite an inheritance! There's too much to relate here so you will have to wait to hear all about it. I can hardly wait to tell you in person... for many reasons...

I know we will be traveling on soon to the town of Alton, Illinois, which is from where Jessie hails. I will, of course, leave an address for you, should we leave prior to your arrival here.

As the days grow shorter, so does the distance between us. I pray for your safe journey and that we be reunited sooner rather than later!

 Until then, I will see you in my dreams...,

Your Mary

COOP

Just got back to the Fort... It's cold out and I'm dusty and tired from a week of scoutin'. As I finished reportin' to the Major, he nodded and thanked me.

"Good job, Martin. The Mess should still be serving supper, why don't you go on over and get something hot to eat and drink," he suggested.

"Yes sir, I will," I turned to leave.

"Oh, Martin, I have a couple letters here for you!"

Letters? For me?

I thanked him as I took my letters and headed for the Mess. They were in Mary's hand-writin'. She had a beautiful, flowy style of penmanship. Funny, just lookin' at the writin' made me happy and excited to get to a seat off by myself and read her words.

When I got to the Mess, they were startin' to clear away the line and the Mess Sgt. Shook his head sayin', "Ya almost missed eatin', boy!"

I smiled and thanked him, as he gave me a hefty helpin' of anythin' left on the line. And there was hot coffee- lots of it! Findin' a quiet spot and takin' a big gulp of coffee, I opened the first letter from the 15th. It felt almost like Christmas when I was a little boy!

Been a long time since I anticipated somethin' this much.

The Journal of Jessie Llewellyn

I am beginning to believe that dealing with the law and lawyers is the most tedious activity known to humankind! I have spent more time in carriages to and from Mr. Sutcliffe's offices than I have in the company of my sister and my fiancé! I have been assiduous in asking questions and getting explanations from Mr. Sutcliffe – he really is quite a dear man, though a bit dry in his manner. My portion of Aunt's estate consists of many investment accounts – he has explained that rather than closing them for the access to the bulk of my investments, I should be wiser to keep the money in those same hands. Apparently, the investments are quite sound and will provide a steady income.

"You will have a good deal of cash, Miss Jessie, from your Aunt's bank accounts and the sale of her home, but cash has a way of disappearing," he said, smiling at me. "I do not wish you to think that I believe you will be reckless, my dear, but it is always a good thing to establish a steady income…one never knows what the future will bring, especially in that wilderness you have chosen to live in!"

I couldn't help laughing, as I'm sure he envisioned bank robbers, Indians, and cattle stampedes as being our daily fare!

"I promise you, Mr. Sutcliffe, I shall not become a spendthrift!" I said, giggling a little, "but I also assure you that my 'wilderness' is really quite civilized! One day you must visit us in Wyoming Territory – we'll make sure you are quite safe!"

He chuckled and said, "My dear Miss Jessie – I may look old and settled, and perhaps as dusty as my law books, but I still enjoy a bit of adventure, now and then!"

"I shall make note of that, sir, and, should you choose to visit, will make arrangements for an adventure or two, just for you!" I said, laughing.

"I shall hold you to that, my dear!" he said, and rose to escort me to his outer office, "Tell that young man of yours I expect him to introduce me to some interesting fellows, when I do come out West!"

"I am sure he'd be delighted to do so, Mr. Sutcliffe," I said, "Just as long as you don't decide to change your profession and join him as a Pinkerton agent – he has trouble enough watching over me!"

"I don't doubt that," my lawyer said, trying to look stern, "just remember, my dear, bravery needs common sense to balance it!"

"I shall, dear sir, and I thank you for all you are doing for me!" I said.

He smiled and said, "I enjoy the novelty of having a client who is more interested in being happy than in being rich! Bless you, my dear!"

MARY

St. Joseph, Missouri

October 23, 1874

My Darling,

It has been slow going here as the heat has become stifling. Because of the unusually hot weather, I have resorted to cooling baths in the afternoons and sitting in my room with the windows open wearing nothing but my shift. I can hardly believe I have put those words on paper, but I suppose it is all right since we *are* affianced! I hope you do not think me brazen...

I am getting a lot of reading done as they have quite a lovely Library here. The selection is wonderful, offering a little something for everyone. Fear not, my dearest, I wore my green cotton dress there!

It is now pouring rain. I hope you are not someplace where the weather is being so fickle. At least the temperature is falling, and it promises to be more temperate tomorrow.

All My Love,

Your Mary

The Journal of Jessie Llewellyn:

My poor Mary! I have been back and forth to Mr. Sutcliffe so often that I have had little time to enjoy her company!

Vin has been busy also with various meetings at the Pinkerton agency....in the evenings, we have been able to dine together with Mary, who has been kind enough to bring me some books from the library. Mr. Sutcliffe has promised that as soon as Aunt's house is sold, we will be free to make our way to Alton.... it is amusing, in a way, my mixed feelings about that! I dread the lectures and recriminations I shall undoubtedly hear, but I can't help giggling, thinking of the surprise and consternation that will ensue when I arrive, an engaged woman - and to such a handsome, exciting man!

VIN

Goodwin came by the hotel yesterday. I was down in the hotel bar havin' a drink while Jessie and Mary went out shoppin'. and I was kinda surprised to see him.

"Hello, Harper," he said, comin' up to the bar beside me.

"Howdy," I said, "care for a drink?"

"Sounds like a good idea," he said, lookin' just a little put out.

"Somethin' on your mind?" I asked, wonderin' what'd got his dander up.

"Yes and no," he said, noddin' at the bartender to leave the bottle.

"Anythin' I can help with?" I asked, sippin' the whiskey he'd poured me.

"Could be," he said, "My boss is worried about you signin' on, Harper."

"How come?" I asked, surprised. I'd met his boss, fella named Grantley, and he seemed right friendly.

"You didn't tell me you'd been jailed in Laramie on a murder charge," Goodwin said, lookin' me in the eye, "Why not?"

I shook my head, thinkin' about that nasty piece of work, Antoinette, and her lies – not real surprised that this had come up.

"Well?" Goodwin asked, kinda impatient like.

"Mainly," I said, lookin' at him straight back, "because I was innocent, and the charge was dismissed."

"I know that," Goodwin said, still impatient, "but Grantley knew about it and I didn't, and I recommended you -how come you didn't tell me up front?"

"Listen, Goodwin," I said, keepin' calm, "You knew I had a reputation – I was up front about that – but I also told you I'd never shot anybody who wasn't shootin' at me. Do you tell your life story to anybody who asks?"

He kinda grinned at that, and I let out a breath. I sure didn't want to punch the guy – I liked him - but I'd come danged close for a minute.

"Sorry, Vin," he said, kinda sheepish, "I just got hot under the collar at Grantley for questioning my judgement and I guess I'm taking it out on you…"

"You tell Grantley to wire the sheriff in Laramie," I said, "I got nothin' to hide. As a matter o' fact, tell him to wire the Federal Marshal in Denver – Jim Abelard. That should settle any doubts he has."

"I'll do that!" he said, really grinnin' this time, "If having a Federal marshal vouch for you doesn't satisfy him, nothing will!"

"Jim's a good man," I said, pouring Goodwin a drink, "and he knows me pretty well…"

"I'll bet he'd have a few stories to tell," Goodwin said, raisin' his glass, "but I'm guessing I won't hear any, unless you tell them!"

"You got that right," I said, grinnin' back, "and I'm not tellin' a damned thing! Might ruin his reputation."

MARY

St. Joseph, Missouri

October 27, 1874

My Darling,

After the recent cold snap, the leaves on the trees have truly begun to take on those beautiful shades of autumn. I have always loved this time of year. Many people are not fond of it as it portends that winter is not far behind... but I see the colors of yellow, red and rust and revel in the beauty of the change of seasons.

I ventured out with Jessie today and came upon a lovely little dress shop. We both found frocks there. Jessie's is in a beautiful shade of blue which highlights her eyes and mine is in a pretty, almost olive green.

How silly you must think I am when you read this. Not much has been happening otherwise, I just wish to relate everything I can as it makes me feel closer to you....

Missing Your Touch,

Your Mary

COOP

I couldn't help but thinkin' about the conversation I'd had with the Major at the beginnin' of the week... the new recruits had arrived, and I asked if I could be released.

"I'm sorry, Martin, but they need to be trained up more before I can discharge you." He smiled then, "Might get out of here faster if you help them along with their education. A lot of them are from back east and have absolutely no clue. As you know, it has only been three-and-a-half months since the Bates Battle massacre on 4 July, and the Indians are still riled."

We had several of those new recruits with us today. Most were pretty green still but there were some who were very promisin'. Two of 'em were brothers who showed a lotta interest in learnin' how to scout. In fact, I had a dozen of the new men out with me this past five days, trainin' them what to look for when scoutin'. I let the brothers take the lead on the return trip while I watched over them. The whole lot were pretty promisin'. I might get released sooner than later at this rate! One could hope…

None of them seemed to mind too much when I suggested we stop at a nearby town, so I could send a telegraph to my Mary, lettin' her know I was delayed. Dadgum, but I hated to disappoint her… or was it *my* disappointment I was feelin'?

The Journal of Jessie Llewellyn

These last few days have been both frustrating and hectic! I have been back and forth to Mr. Sutcliffe's office repeatedly, signing this and signing that- fortunately, I read quickly, as I am not fool enough to sign anything without reading it! He has put Aunt's house up for sale and there are several interested parties, so it appears that the house will be sold before the end of the month, thank fortune.

Coop has not yet arrived in St. Joseph, but Mary has taken to leaving dated letters at the Wagon Train headquarters since they know him there so that when he does arrive, he will know if we have left for Alton. Vin ran into some difficulty with the Pinkerton Agency over the murder charge of which he was acquitted, but telegrams flew between here and various law enforcement officers and it has been resolved. I know he was concerned about it, but being Vin, he concealed it under a mask of humor, saying, "Don't fret, little girl- sooner or later, they'll straighten it out and the

lawmen know me well enough by now to expect this kinda thing!"

When I looked at him with surprise, he responded, "I've had my share of scrapes, mi corazon, but I've made quite a few friends along the way." He grinned, and said, "Pays to have friends, honey- never know when you'll need 'em!"

"I'll remember that, dearest, and cultivate some sheriffs for myself!" I replied.

He laughed and gave me a hug, but said, seriously, "I'm hopin' you don't need 'em for this kinda thing, little girl!"

"One never knows!" I said, smiling mischievously, "I'm not exactly a timid rabbit any more, Vin!"

He looked a little alarmed and put his hands on my shoulders. "Little girl, don't tempt fate - she has a tendency to bite!"

MARY

"Miss McDonnaugh?"

I turned to the clerk at the hotel desk. "Yes?"

"A telegram just arrived for you," he said as he handed it to me.

Excitedly, I took it and opened the paper. Anticipating good news, I looked over at Jessie, "It's from Coop!" and I began to read. Sighing, I shared the news with her, "He's going to be late."

Bless her, realizing how dejected this news made me feel, she just put an arm around me and gave me a gentle squeeze, "It won't be too much longer, honey, I'm sure, or he would have certainly mentioned if he would be delayed more than a few days…"

"I suppose…" Then, "We head for Alton when your aunt's house sells?"

She smiled, "We head for Alton as soon as the house sells."

COOP

Headin' back to the Fort with a contingent of soldiers, we had to pass near a town so small that basically all they had was a tiny school house, a black smith's, a sheriff, a telegraph office and a saloon. It didn't take much convincin' by the men for the Sergeant to allow us to stop and 'water the horses'. Of course, the best water trough seemed to be right in front of that saloon…

Before anyone was allowed in, Sgt. Whaley laid down the law and ordered his men to behave and be ready to leave in an hour, no more.

Followin' Ed into the establishment, I waved to the bartender for a couple beers, my treat. Ed had wrangled a table while I was waitin' for our beers over at the bar when a sweet young thing walked over to me.

"Mister? You lookin' for a good time?"

I had to do a double-take. She couldn't've been more than fifteen years old!

"Ain't you a little young to be workin' in a saloon?"

"It's a small town, mister, and all my folks're dead. A girl does what she has too, if you know what I mean." That last part had been whispered in my ear.

One of the Privates came over and runnin' a hand down her arm, said, "He has a gal, but I don't! How about you and me go upstairs?"

I was about ready to step in when she replied, "It'll cost extra."

Shakin' my head, I took our beers over to the table. I wondered what led women into that kinda life. Not bein' a saloon hostess, that's an honest livin', but sellin' your body like that… don't know why it bothered me so much… guess I wondered at the dire straits that changed her life to this course…

"You thinkin' about your girl again?"

"What? Naw, just contemplatin'…"

"Well, it shouldn't be much longer before those new recruits are settled in and the Major lets you go. You must be lookin' forward to that."

"You just don't know, Ed. You just don't know." I felt that smile I get whenever I think on my Mary. "I can't believe how much I've missed her," I admitted out loud.

The Journal of Jessie Llewellyn

Aunt Martha's house has been sold! That was the last thing for which my signature will be needed, so we should be able to leave for Alton day after tomorrow! No sign of Coop, as yet, but Mary assures me that she will leave word for him at the wagon train offices before we leave, letting him know where we will be. I feel a bit guilty in delaying her own travel to Virginia for so long, but she has been so helpful and encouraging that I am also very glad she has been here with us!

Now that my business is almost concluded and the Pinkertons

have been satisfied regarding my beloved's character and suitability, the next hurdle will be our visit with Mama and Papa. We will stay in a hotel in Alton, as it is only about a half hour buggy ride to their house from the city, thus we will then not be imposing upon them, nor will I be bored to death with the daily company of my sisters!! I hope that Coop will soon be joining us - mostly for Mary's sake, but Vin and I are looking forward to seeing him as well! After all, Coop is now my family, too!

MARY

St. Joseph, Missouri

October 29, 1874

My Love,

Tomorrow we are to take the morning train to Alton, Illinois, as Jessie's aunt's house has sold quicker than any of us anticipated. We plan to stay at the Grand Hotel there, and I will leave word for you at the desk as the days go by; as we may remain there for a while.

I believe that Jessie is a bit nervous regarding the visit with her family although she is looking forward to 'showing Vin off,' as she puts it, to her parents and her siblings. I, personally, would give anything to see their faces as her parents meet Vin and see the changes in their daughter. She certainly has blossomed into a vibrant, self-confident young woman. From what she has told me, her family will not be too thrilled with her being able to think for herself! They are somewhat stodgy, to say the least, and women are to be seen, more as decoration, and bear and raise the children, not needing, or expected to be able to think for themselves. How boring! I am so glad that my future husband isn't intimidated by a woman with a brain.

Please be safe, dearest, I am discovering that there are fewer like you and Vin out there than I thought!

I cannot wait until we are reunited.

Forever Yours,

Mary

The Journal of Jessie Llewellyn

At least our train trip to St. Louis did not include a robbery! We took the ferry across the river and it was cooler on the water and there was a breeze. I had forgotten the humid heat of my former home during the summers and the drastic changes of seasons during my time in Wyoming- how I miss that lovely wilderness!

We have checked into the Grand Hotel and plan to rest this evening - Mary has sent a message to the wagon train office with the name of our hotel so Coop, who had still not arrived when we left St. Joseph, will know where to find us.

We will visit Mama and Papa tomorrow. I shall need a good dinner this evening and a good night's rest to prepare for that encounter! Mary and I again share a room, with Vin directly across the hall from us. We shall meet in the lobby shortly for dinner in the hotel dining room. Perhaps showing up on Mama's and Papa's doorstep without advance notice was not the best plan I ever made, but the consequences could have been much more dire than they actually were!

Vin had asked me last night at dinner if I wished him to don a suit for the visit and I was adamant! "Don't you dare! Unless you want me to divorce you even before we are married! I had more than enough of men in 'city suits' when I lived here!"

He looked a bit surprised, and perhaps rueful, so I decided to modify my prohibition.

"If you really want to, my dearest," I said, relenting a bit because he looked so startled at my tone and expression, "please do, but don't think you have to in order to please me or anyone else! I fell in love with *you*, my heart, not your attire!" I did not say it, although I thought it, "That attire helped, dear man, especially the well-fitting jeans!"

"I'd be more comfortable without the suit, mi corazon, I just didn't want your folks to think you'd be marryin' a grubby ranch hand!" he grinned.

"If they were marrying you, it might matter, but since I'm the one who is, you are most pleasing to the eye even when you are soaking wet and muddy!" I said, forcefully.

He laughed at that and said, "Well, little girl, if you feel that way maybe I should arrange to fall into a mud puddle on the way to your folks' place!"

Mary, who had been stifling her laughter all throughout this exchange, finally gave up trying and started to giggle so infectiously that I soon joined her!

As it turned out, when Mama opened the door to us, she was so very startled that she barely recognized me, let alone noticed Vin or Mary. Once she realized it really was her errant daughter, she hugged me and gave me a kiss on the cheek, exclaiming, "Jessie! Where on earth have you been?"

It seemed an odd thing to say, but I just said, "In Wyoming, Mama, and lately in St. Joseph, Missouri."

Mama remembered her matronly duties and invited all of us into the parlor, where Papa was rising from his easy chair, probably to inspect improper visitors before Mama allowed them into the house.

"Mama, Papa, I'd like you to meet my dear friend, Miss Mary McDonnaugh, and my fiancé, Mr. Vin Harper." I said, indicating my companions. Mama promptly fainted, and Papa, being apparently too stunned to move, would have let her fall if my Vin had not, with his cat-like grace, caught her before she hit the floor! Once we had revived Mama and unfrozen Papa, I performed the introductions over again as I was not sure either of them had taken anything in completely. We were all seated in the parlor, making conversation (somewhat heavy going, as Mama seemed fascinated by Vin and Papa was most taken with Mary!), when I decided it was time to get down to business and told my parents about Aunt Martha's estate and my decisions thereto. Papa was aghast, (his expression so mirroring Mr. Sutcliffe's that I didn't dare look at Vin for fear both of us would explode with laughter) and attempted, with no success, to dissuade me from "throwing away a fortune." I repeatedly told him that even were I so inclined, the dispositions had already been made, but Papa was his usual self- hearing only what he wished to hear and sure that he knew best.

Once Mama perceived that I was becoming a bit angry, she

stepped in and said, "I will see that the maid prepares rooms for you all," and started to rise from her seat on the sofa.

"No need, Mama," I said, before she was all the way up and scurrying for the maid (for a woman of advancing years Mama can move as quickly as a squirrel sighting a large nut when she chooses to!). "Mary, Vin, and I are at the Grand Hotel in Alton for the duration of our stay. We are awaiting the arrival of Mary's fiancé, Mr. Cooper Martin, within the next day or two, and Mary must travel on to her home in Virginia to conduct some family business very soon."

Mama looked a bit relieved, although she maintained her hostess demeanor, and said, "But it is no trouble, Jessie- we'd love to have all of you with us! Your sisters and their families surely will want to see you and meet your... friends!"

That slight hesitation gave me pause- knowing Mama, I foresaw a conference with Papa regarding the suitability of a "cowboy" as a son-in-law, and, out of part filial devotion and part self-preservation, I proceeded to rise and indicate our immediate departure. "We will be in Alton for at least a few days, Mama," I said, "I'm sure you will want to arrange a little get-together to welcome Vin to our family. You can send us a message at the hotel when you are ready..." I then gave her and Papa a kiss each, and walked toward the door, Mary and Vin, having risen when I did, said their goodbyes and expressed their pleasure at meeting my parents, and then followed me out the front door.

I turned and waved at Mama and Papa standing on the porch.

Papa had his arm around Mama's shoulders, and she was waving weakly at me and saying, "Goodbye, dear- we will send a message to you as soon as plans for a proper engagement party are made."

MARY

The ride back to Alton began quietly enough. It had been an… interesting meeting, to say the least. Vin looked over at Jessie who seemed lost in thought. Then he knocked her knee with his. This caught her attention as she turned and smiled at him. At this point, I had to laugh out loud when he very slowly raised his hand and deliberately flicked her shoulder with his forefinger! She immediately flicked him back!

"Don't make me separate the two of you," I said, laughing still.

Following Vin's ice breaker (he always seems to know how to cheer Jessie), we ended up talking all the way back to town. First about her parents' reactions, then speculating on what they would be telling her siblings, wondering if her father would attempt to interfere in any manner with her decision regarding the inheritance, although this seemed quite impossible, but he may try. We also wondered about the engagement party. I so hoped my Coop would be there in time to enjoy the festivities because I am fairly certain that night would be one to remember!

Upon our return to the hotel, I excused myself as I knew Jessie and Vin would like some time to themselves before retiring for the evening, and it gave me a chance to write another letter for my beloved, telling him all about meeting Jessie's parents and their reactions, especially to Vin.

The Journal of Jessie Llewellyn

Today we had our first "family visit" with my eldest sister, Emily, and her husband, Tom Marshall. He is a lawyer, but not as kind as Mr. McKenzie or Mr. Sutcliffe. Tom has always been a bit pompous, and he has deteriorated considerably in that same direction over the months that I have been gone! He shook hands with Vin, uttered a sound something like 'Ummph,' then seated himself on the most comfortable chair in the hotel lobby alcove and said nothing for the rest of the visit - probably the best outcome! I will admit that their sons, George, Elliot, and Fred, are nice looking boys and considerably more well -mannered than their parents! As I expected, they were instantly enamored of my Vin, and plied him with questions about the Wild West.

"Did you shoot many Indians, sir?" asked George (the eldest).

"Well, son, only enough to get by," was Vin's answer.

Then Elliot chimed in, "How about outlaws, sir?"

"A couple," Vin said, grinning, "but they deserved it!"

Last, but not least, Fred demanded to see Vin's "six gun" and Vin, bless him, showed the boy his pistol, explaining that they were not to touch it, but letting them see how it worked and how the bullets were loaded. The boys were as thrilled as if my beloved were a one-man circus!

Their parents, however, seemed both fascinated and repulsed by the "bloodthirsty" questions the boys had for Vin, and Emily, sotto voce, asked me, "Does he really kill people?" She looked both avid and terrified, so I couldn't help myself!

"Only when they annoy him too much." I said, demurely. "I, on the other hand, only shoot people when I have to." I thought Emily would emulate Mama and drop in a dead faint, but she recovered enough to indicate to Tom that they should be going, expressing, rather insincerely, her pleasure in meeting my intended and her hopes that we should get together again soon. By the time they left, Vin was regarding me with a quizzical expression, and I knew I was in for it!

We moved to a secluded corner of the lobby and he asked, "What did you tell your sister, little girl? I was showin' the boys my gun and couldn't quite hear."

"Why do you ask?" I said, trying to maintain a straight face.

"She looked like a scared mouse runnin' away from a tiger when she left," he said, rather severely.

"Not much," I said, stifling a giggle, "Just that you only shoot people who annoy you too much and I only do it when necessary,"

I couldn't hold in my giggles any longer and Vin came over and grabbed me, sitting down and holding me on his lap, and said, "You, my little hellcat, are scarier than a pack of screamin' Comanches!"

I couldn't stop laughing, and he kissed me (most thoroughly!) before saying, "Little girl, are you tryin' to convince your family that you are some kind o' crazy?"

"Actually love, I guess I am!" I said, realizing that was just what I was trying to do! "You see, love, they already think I'm just too odd' for comfort and will try to make me realize that I need to conform to their view of what I should be. I want to convince them
that it's not even possible, let alone desirable!"

"I think I understand, mi corazon," he said, after a little thought, "you're doin' your best to keep 'em from tryin' to put you back in that cage again. I don't think they could, darlin', but they do, so you go right ahead and have fun convincin' them that you are beyond redemption! I can see you're havin' fun doin' it and I don't blame you, if all of 'em are as stuffy as that pair!"

He grinned at me, and I snuggled close, regardless of the fact, that we were in full view of the desk clerk. "Thank you, dearest love, " I whispered, "I've finally learned to laugh at them instead of fear and dread their disapproval."

MARY

Over dinner this evening, Jessie and Vin related the tale of the first of her relatives to visit. Vin could hardly resist laughing aloud when he mentioned the various questions Jessie's nephews asked him. Who would have thought that a man with his past could be so patient with youngsters… Jessie told me how she feels so much freer of spirit, knowing that she made the right decision when she fled her family and headed west.

I remember the girl I met last spring and how much she has blossomed since leaving her family… how much happier she is, especially since finding her Vin… Oh, but it was truly a blessed day when we all crossed each other's paths!

The Journal of Jessie Llewellyn

Apparently, word has gotten around, at least among my nephews, of "Auntie Jessie's cowboy."

Mary, Vin and I had just returned from luncheon at a local

restaurant and were entering the hotel, when the desk clerk beckoned to me. I walked to the main desk and he said, "Miss Llewellyn, there are some people here to see you. They are in the dining room, as I told them you were out - they asked me to request that you join them. I believe they are members of your family."

Bracing myself for the onslaught, I walked back to Vin and Mary and said, "Another delightful visit from some of my family is in the offing - would you two please join us in the dining room?"

Vin grinned at me and said, "Sure, little girl, lookin' forward to meetin' more of 'em." Mary looked a bit apprehensive, as I had told her about Emily's visit yesterday, but, dear girl that she is, she decided to come along.

This time it was my sister, Hortense, and her husband, Paul Ames- and, of course, their twins, Andrew and John. We joined them at a large table to the rear of the dining room and introductions were made.

Paul seized Vin by the hand and began pumping it as if he were drawing water for a sink full of dirty dishes and boomed, oozing good fellowship, "Glad to meet you, Mr. Harper! You must come by my dry goods store one day- got some very fine suits that would just 'suit' you!" This was followed by a wink and a hearty laugh.

Meanwhile, Hortense was eyeing Mary's and my frocks between sideways simpering glances at Vin.

"Oh, dear Mr. Harper, " she crooned, fluttering her eyelashes, "How very handsome you are! I always thought that Jessie would remain a spinster, but I can see why I was wrong!"

For a moment, I thought Vin was going to say something, but he just smiled and took her offered hand. The twins placed themselves on either side of Vin and began clamoring to see the "six gun" their cousins had bragged about, while my poor Vin attempted to explain that the hotel dining room was not really a suitable place for examining firearms.

Hortense giggled and said, "Oh, dear Mr. Harper- our boys would be so disappointed! Their cousins have told them so much about you and boys will be boys... "

Vin looked at me and shrugged, saying, "Yes, ma'am, I'll take the boys up to my room if that's OK by you?"

"Why of course," she responded (with more eyelash activity), "I just know they'll be perfectly safe with you!"

"Great," boomed Paul, "When you get back, we'll talk about your coming to work for me! You'd make a crackerjack clerk! The ladies would flock to my establishment!"

Vin looked very startled, and then began to chuckle. "I've been told that before, sir," he said, smiled at me, and herded Andrew and John out of the room.

"Mama said, Miss McDonnaugh, that you are from Virginia, I believe?" said Hortense, with no simper and no fluttering of lashes as Vin was now out of sight.

"Yes, I am," said Mary, smiling politely.

"Did the men in your family go to war on the Rebel side, then?" Hortense asked, archly.

Mary replied quietly, "Yes, ma'am - I lost two brothers in the war."

Hortense continued, "My Paul was in the Union army- he mustered out as a lieutenant. We are all very proud of him!"

I could see that this was a painful subject for Mary, so before Hortense could continue her saga of Paul and the War, I said, as admiringly as I could, "Hortense, the boys seem to have grown a foot since I left!"

She immediately turned her attention to me and began telling me all of their exploits and virtues while I did my best to appear fascinated. Mary threw me a look of gratitude and began talking with Paul about his store, a subject dear to his heart. Vin and the boys came back very soon after that, and their parents took their leave within a few minutes, having many important calls to make that afternoon, according to Hortense.

By the time Mary and I got to our room (Vin said he was going to visit the saloon bar in the hotel- he looked as if he might need something for "medicinal purposes" so I had no objection!), we were almost helpless with laughter. Once we had divested ourselves of hats and dresses and were in our shifts (it was an usually muggy day and we were both very warm!), I said, "Mary, Hortense doesn't even know how to spell 'tact,' let alone possess any!"

Mary smiled and said, "Honey, I could tell!"

That set us off again! Finally, we were both ready to stretch out for a rest.

"Now would be the time for some of your 'medicinal' coffee!" I said.

Mary asked, "How many more sisters do you have, honey? I want to be prepared!"

"If I tell you, promise you won't run away?" I said with a grimace.

"I won't desert you, honey," she laughed, "just so the number is under ten!"

VIN

Once the girls had gone upstairs, I headed straight for the bar – I was right tempted to order a bottle, but I figgered I'd be better off takin' one glass at a time! My poor little girl! Aint' no wonder she wanted to escape from her family!

I ain't usually comfortable bein' down on anybody's family (mine ain't all that shinin' an example) but if I'd had to live with those sisters and their husbands I'd likely be in jail! Those twins o' her sisters are a handful – I practically had to tie 'em down to get 'em settled! Once they got to see my gun and hear all about the "Wild West" they quieted down some, but it seemed to me that they'd been told so often how wonderful they was by their Mama that good manners just didn't matter!! We had a bit of a tussle there for a while – both of 'em mighta benefitted from a trip to the woodshed, but they ain't mine, thank God, so I just growled a bit and they started actin' a little better. I ain't been ogled by a woman like that Hortense in polite company afore – mostly that kinda outright flirtin' comes from the dance hall gals!

I thought hard about gettin' that bottle, but I knew we'd have more of Jessie's relations showin' up tomorrow and havin' a hangover wasn't a real good idea!

The Journal of Jessie Llewellyn

Mary, Vin, and I dined in the hotel this evening. We were speculating upon the likelihood of Coop arriving tomorrow when our waiter brought a note to me at our table. It was from my sister, Serena (apparently the "sister brigade" decided to visit in descending order of age!), who, with her husband, Adam Kennedy, and their two boys, Michael and Edward, were awaiting us in the lobby.

When I imparted this news to Vin and Mary and asked for their company, they looked at one another with almost identical expressions of mild alarm. "I can't promise you'll enjoy it," I said, apologetically, "but it's best to get it over with!"

Vin squeezed my hand, smiled, and said in that lovely deep voice, "Little girl, if you can stand it, Mary and I can - I've faced worse!"

Mary grinned and said, "After all, honey, like it or not, they're family!"

With a resigned sigh, I arose and led the way to the lobby. Serena gave me a perfunctory hug and introduced herself and the boys to Mary. Adam, eyeing Vin's height (Adam is about 5'6" tall), unconsciously rose a bit on his toes and shook hands with me and then with Vin.

"Just what is your profession, Mr. Harper?" he inquired, in a manner that suggested Vin was an applicant for a loan at Adam's bank (he is a clerk and has aspirations to an executive position, apparently still unfulfilled). Vin looked a little disconcerted - such inquiries are considered ill-mannered in the West - but replied, courteously, "You might say, sir, that I am in the security business."

"Security, eh? I understood from my papa-in-law that you were a cowboy- is that not a type of manual laborer on some sort of cattle farm?"

I could see Vin struggling to hold in a laugh, but he lost the fight and grinned widely, saying, "We call it a ranch, mister, and security could be called 'manual labor' as I often need to use my gun hand to provide it!"

Adam cleared his throat, stepped back a pace and gestured to the group of chairs and sofas near us in the lobby. "Let's have a seat. Ladies, if you will..."

Serena took the boys by the hands and seated herself on the sofa with one on either side of her. Mary and I chose two chairs and Vin and Adam remained standing. Michael and Edward looked a bit like startled owls- eyes wide and fixed on Vin in fascinated stares. I knew they were longing to ask him about "cowboy" life, but their mama had a firm grip on each, so they were forced to content themselves with staring.

The rest of our "conversation" revolved around Mary's family and their social and financial status, my foolishness regarding Aunt's inheritance, and further inquiries into just how much Vin earned as "security" on a "cattle farm."

After a half hour of this, I rose and said, "Serena, Adam – we have so enjoyed your company, but we are planning to visit several saloons this evening and must freshen up before we leave. The boys must be tired as well! I'm sure we will all see one another again before Mary must depart for Virginia. Give Mama and Papa my love!"

They rose and after another handshake for Vin from Adam and a feeble hug for me from Serena, they departed.

Vin looked at me and said, "Saloons, little girl?" with that unruly eyebrow raised, "just what saloons are we visitin'?"

Mary looked about to burst, so I said, contritely, "None that I know of, my dear, but I just couldn't stand another minute of that, and hoped we'd be spared further 'conversation,' at least!"

"Well, mi corazon, my guess is that your mama and papa are goin' to get an earful when sister Serena gets ahold of 'em!" Vin said.

"You know, Jessie," said Mary, between giggles, "I really do understand your desire to go West- if I were you, I'd consider China!"

MARY

Alton, Illinois

November 5, 1874

Oh My Dearest,

I have met Jessie's parents and now three of her four sisters, their spouses and children. I understand her need to travel West as she did. Let's just say that I cannot wait for you to be introduced to them all as there are no words to describe them. How she turned out the way she did amazes me! It is a testament to her strong determination and fierce intellect, I believe.

I find myself wondering at her family, as the dynamic is so very different from that of my own… we all acted in the best interests of each other… supportive… To witness such reactions as exhibited by her parents and siblings is boggling to my mind.

I am eager for the day you arrive, as I miss you terribly…

All My Love,

Your Mary

The Journal of Jessie Llewellyn

We all rested well last night, in spite of our "delightful" visit from Serena and were just arising from breakfast in the hotel dining room when the waiter delivered a missive, this time from my youngest sister, Alice. She and her minister husband, Roger Squires (he is curate at one of the churches in Alton and, as I remember, quite a "serious" young man!), were in the lobby waiting to see us. Just the two of them- they most obligingly left their two-year-old son, Roger, Jr., at home under the care of one of the members of the Ladies' Aid Society! When we reached the lobby, I realized Alice had "news" for me, as she was quite obviously with child to such an extent that I feared the lobby might witness the birth!

After introductions all around, we seated ourselves (I am beginning to believe that the desk clerk has hung a discreet "reserved" sign on the settee and chairs in that portion of the lobby!), and Alice smiled coyly at Vin, placing her hands on her abdominal region, and said, "Just think, Mr. Harper, you may be a godfather very soon!"

Vin actually gulped, and the expression on his face beggared description!

Mary discreetly hid her grin behind her hand, and I cannot say that I did not roll my eyes to Heaven at that "honor" being conferred upon my Vin!

Vin recovered himself sufficiently to say, most gallantly, "I'd be honored, ma'am, but right now Jessie's and my plans are not yet settled and I'm not sure how long we'll be here in your fair city."

My brother-in-law harrumphed and proceeded to inquire into Vin's and Mary's religious affiliations- I suppose with a view to gathering them into his "flock" as soon as possible.

Alice sat, looking a bit uncomfortable, as the settee had a straight back and sitting upright in her condition was nigh impossible. I felt sorry for her but wasn't about to go into it as I knew I would hear every detail of her increasing girth and sensations, as I had before Roger, Jr's birth. It was not a subject in which I had any deep interest, preferring to avoid the recitation, if possible!

While her husband was interrogating Vin and Mary, I did ask her when she expected her confinement, which was a mistake, as she began to reminisce about that event with Roger, Jr.! I jumped in as soon as I could, and said, "Are you hoping for another son, Alice, or a daughter?"

"Oh, my, Jessie!" she exclaimed, "How could I hope for anything but another son! Daughters are so often disappointing!"

This was said with a sidelong glance at Vin and a smirk.

"Very true," I replied, "they sometimes develop minds of their own and cause all sorts of problems for their families!"

Vin overheard my remark, which, I blush to confess, was uttered a bit acidly, but instead of reproach, he grinned at me and mouthed "hellcat" under his breath! I almost burst into laughter but managed to control myself long enough to bring this current "delightful" visit to a close without further disaster!

Once Alice and Roger had wended their ponderous (at least on Alice's part!) way out the hotel doors, I breathed an enormous sigh of relief and said to Mary and Vin, "Thank heavens that's the last of them!"

Vin came to me, put his arms around me, and kissed me soundly. Once I had recovered breath enough to speak, I said, "I thoroughly enjoyed that, love, but what was the reason for it?"

"Little girl," he said, "how in hell did you manage to turn out so fine?"

I giggled, and said, "Just the luck of the draw, dear heart - if it hadn't been for Aunt Martha, I might have been a pale copy of one of them!"

"Then God bless Aunt Martha, wherever she is!" he exclaimed, "I owe her more than I could ever pay! She musta been quite a lady!"

"She was," I said, a little sadly, "I wish you could have met her."

"Me, too, mi corazon, but I figure I got a little piece of her in you." he said, holding me close.

I couldn't help dampening his shirt again, just a little- how I love this man!

Mary came over and patted my arm, saying, "Honey, you amaze me. I was beginning to think I ought to hide your pistol somewhere, but you came off with flying colors."

We all laughed, mostly from relief, but overjoyed that the "sister brigade" had finally finished their onslaught!

MARY

Alton, Illinois

November 8, 1874

Good Morning, My Dearest,

Having had a dream of you I awakened early before Jessie, or anyone else in town, it seems. It was such of a lovely thing... I could hear your voice and almost feel your touch as I awoke… I am hoping this means you are not far distant!

Vin and I have now met all of Jessie's family, the youngest appearing yesterday afternoon. It is truly amazing how patient Vin is with the children who are so very excited to meet a "real, live cowboy!" Although he lost a bit of his composure when a very pregnant Alice alluded to him becoming godfather to the soon-to-be newest member of the clan! The look on his face was priceless.

I will close now and hope and pray to see you soon.

I'll Love You,

Forever and a day,

Your Mary

The Journal of Jessie Llewellyn

I thought I was accurate in stating that my family had completed their mission to annoy me, at least at the hotel, but Mama and Papa decided to pay us a visit yesterday! I have been a bit of a sluggard this morning- Mary was up and moving long before I drifted up out of sleep. Having to deal with my parents was more of an ordeal than all my sisters and their appendages combined! It took me quite a while to compose myself for sleep, as I was unable to walk about in the cool mountain evenings I miss so much. A city is not the best place for an unaccompanied woman to take an evening stroll - there may be more coyotes, wolves, and screech owls haunting the Wyoming nights, but far fewer human predators than in a city!

Ostensibly, my parents came to the hotel to tell us of the "party" planned for tomorrow- a "gathering of the clan," as if having to deal with Emily, Hortense, Serena, and Alice, their husbands, and their interesting offspring individually were not enough! At any rate, after Papa spent more than forty-five minutes questioning my sanity regarding Aunt's inheritance, and Mama kept casting anxious glances at Vin, as if she expected him to start firing his pistol at the desk clerk or bursting into a Comanche war whoop, they finally got around to letting us know that a celebration of my engagement was planned. Mama was swift to inform me that "simply everyone" would be there to welcome Vin to the family.

Dread filled my soul, and I seriously considered coming down with some loathsome disease that would require my immediate departure for a sanitarium! My dearest Vin was my rock, and Mary reassured me that she would be by my side to divert anyone I might want to shoot, so I have resigned myself to the inevitable and plan to shop for a becoming frock with Mary this afternoon. I am sorely tempted to seek out one that would befit a "saloon girl," but that would reflect poorly on my beloved, so I shall resist the temptation!

I am a bit concerned about one thing that arose during our visit with Mama and Papa, though. Papa said something about "seeking aid" from Mr. Sutcliffe, Aunt Martha's lawyer, but I don't recall in what context, as I was doing my utmost to ignore most of what he said lest I disgrace myself in public by screaming at him! On reflection, I have no idea why he would need aid from Aunt's lawyer, as he has his own attorney here in Alton. I trust Mr. Sutcliffe, but I wonder if I should make a point of telegraphing him, just in case. Ah, well, perhaps Coop will arrive in time for the party - with the cousins so closely resembling one another, it might make for a bit of amusement in what promises to be an exercise in exerting iron control over my temper and smilingly enduring two or three hours of deadly boredom!

COOP

Mary wasn't at the hotel, dang it… the clerk handed me a couple letters addressed to me… after readin' 'em and still no sign of her, I thought I'd just head out and try to find her.

Find her I did! Lordy, but she was a sight... wearin' a brown skirt and a rust colored top with little yella dots on it...payin' attention to some horse hockey in the street... I grabbed that gal and surprised her with a kiss!

What a response! She began to fight me off, even raisin' a small hand to strike a blow, until she discovered it was I who was kissin' her! The kiss, in response, was sure worth waitin' for… I couldn't take my eyes off her and I couldn't let her go… I know I said somethin' but don't rightly remember what... I think my cousin said somethin' but I didn't really hear… or care… the only thing I wanted to do right then was marry that gal… well, that and other things…when I suggested a Justice of the Peace she surprised me by noddin'!

MARY

After finding a lovely dress in shades of a light brown, which almost appeared to be bronze, for Jessie's engagement party, Jessie, Vin and I had just finished a very late lunch at a local cafe. On our way back to the hotel, my attention was diverted by a rather large horse offering in the middle of the street. I found myself in a man's arms being kissed rather thoroughly! Bringing my hands up between us to put some distance there, and then prepare to slap the fiend, I discovered to my complete delight that it was my Coop!

"Oh, Coop!" I managed around another more thorough kiss in which I reciprocated whole-heartedly. Rather breathlessly, and melting against his chest, I sighed, "I thought you would never get here!"

"I took as many trains as I could to get here as fast as I could. I stopped in St. Jo and have been readin' your letters over and over on the way to sustain me," he said, smiling, reaching to move a wayward strand of hair, which had blown across my eyes.

I laughed, "I'm sure the news of my new hat made for thrilling reading."

"Actually," he bent to whisper into my ear, "the one that spurred me on was the image of you layin' naked in the bath tryin' to stay cool!"

Blushing furiously, I was caught up in that brilliant azure gaze, unable to look away even if my life depended upon it. There was a brightness, an intensity, if you will, that I had only had brief glimpses of in the days prior to his leaving... My breath became rapid as my heart beat faster... all I could see was my Coop... I couldn't let go for fear my legs wouldn't support me.

I barely heard Vin greet his cousin, "What took ya so long?"

Not breaking eye contact, Coop dismissed his cousins' question and instead asked, "What time is it?"

Jessie supplied the answer, "Almost 4:30."

"Where's the Justice of the Peace?"

I inhaled, and Coop just smiled, a questioning eyebrow raised. Returning his smile, I nodded assent!

"Just behind you to your left," said a bewildered Vin.

Turning, Coop grabbed my hand and strode with such purpose that I almost had to run to keep up! As we approached the office, there was a man just turning the key to close up for the day.

Somewhat breathlessly Coop managed, "Are you the Justice of the Peace?"

Taken a bit by surprise by the appearance of the four of us at his door, he reacted with raised brows, pushing his spectacles up on his nose and replied in the affirmative.

"We want to get married!"

"Well, that's wonderful," the man replied, sounding truly happy about it. "I can fit you in tomorrow morning. Will ten o'clock be good for you?"

Taking hold of the man's arm, Coop stated emphatically, "We want to be married, *now*!"

Looking down to our clasped hands and Coop's death grip then up at me, he asked, "Are you sure, Miss?"

"Oh, yes! Please!"

"It won't be anything very special as I was on my way out... Only a very quick ceremony..." he responded somewhat disappointedly and apologetically.

"The quicker, the better!" Coop replied.

Shaking his head, he reopened the office door, as we all followed him back inside. "Please tell me your names, and I assume that these are the witnesses?" he asked, waving towards Jessie and Vin.

We provided the information and he began, "Dearly Beloved...." When Coop made a "hurry up" gesture with his hand, the clerk sighed, "Do you James Cooper Martin take-"

"Yes!"

Ahem... "Do you Mary Mason McDonnaugh take this man-"

"I do!"

Another sigh... resignedly, he finished, "I now pronounce you man and wife."

Coop brought those beautiful, strong hands up to cup my face ever so tenderly, bending his head to kiss my lips. The kiss began soft and gentle but developed into something with a life all its own, leaving us both breathless!

We turned to exit and the officiate stopped us, saying, "It's not official without your signatures!"

Having been pointed in the direction of the Certificate, Coop signed something which looked like a spider, in the midst of death-throes, had crawled across the paper before I affixed my own signature, "Mary McDonnaugh Martin." Martin….

"Come *on, darlin'*!" Coop took my hand and led the way to the hotel.

"Wait! That will be $2.00!" cried the officiate at our retreating backs.

"Here ya go," I heard Vin drawl. "Our weddin' gift!" he said with a wink as he and Jessie witnessed the paper.

We fairly ran to the hotel, my hand clasped in Coop's.

Arriving at the desk, Coop stated, "We'd like a room."

"I'm very sorry, sir, but we just filled the last vacancy," replied the clerk.

Thinking fast Coop said, "Then give us the keys to Vin Harper's room. He's my cousin."

We managed to climb the stairs in as close to a controlled manner as possible, but when we turned at the landing, Coop lifted me into his arms and sprinted two steps at a time! Pausing at the door he again kissed me passionately. His hand shook so hard I had to help him fit the key into the lock! Then we were…. inside…

The Journal of Jessie Llewellyn

Mary and her Coop have beaten us back to the hotel - they must have run the whole way! I am so very happy for her. I think I shall never see a more wonderful wedding than their almost incoherent vows in the Justice of the Peace's office, as Vin and I stood up for them, both feeling as if we had been caught up in a whirlwind named Cooper Martin!

When we arrived at the hotel, after a more sedate walk, the desk clerk beckoned to Vin. When we reached the desk, the clerk leaned in toward us and said, almost in a whisper, "Mr. Harper, a gentleman with a young lady just took the key to your room. I hesitated to give it to him, but I felt that he would not have appreciated any delay, and, as we are full up, and he did say he was your cousin, I complied with his request. He and the lady have gone upstairs - I hope I have not created any difficulties for you?"

Vin and I looked at one another and burst out laughing, leaving the poor clerk even more confused than he was already! By the time we sobered enough to reassure the man that the gentleman was indeed Vin's cousin, and the lady was his wife, the clerk smiled and said, again most confidentially, "I do understand, sir, and I am glad to have been of assistance!"

We nearly started laughing uncontrollably again but managed to stifle it until we were out of earshot! We decided to visit the saloon bar in the hotel to see if we could order two bottles of wine to be sent to my room later (we made a point of telling the bartender that it was to be delivered after seven pm!). The bartender assured us it would be done as we requested, so Vin and I decided to purchase some small items of food and beverages for a light supper later.

As we walked, arm in arm, with our packages, Vin looked down at me with a huge grin. "Little girl," he said, "Looks like I'll have to sleep someplace besides my hotel room tonight!"

I looked up at those sparkling blue eyes and replied, "You are a devil, Vin Harper, and I am absolutely delighted!"

"Your mama and papa will have somethin' else to celebrate, mi corazon, at their hoedown tomorrow!" Vin said, chuckling.

"Yes, indeed," I replied, "and we'll have our own celebration in my room tonight!"

"Do we have to wait until tonight to celebrate, mi corazon?" Vin said, his eyes twinkling even more.

"Not if you'd rather avoid postponing it," I said, laughter bubbling up inside me (along with many other feelings!).

"Not a minute longer than it takes us to climb the stairs," he said, laughing, and we increased our pace. I think I have forgotten how to blush, but I do not care!!

MARY

We awoke several times during the night, enjoying each other's company in our marriage bed. It seems my Coop knows more about my body than I do after living in it for twenty-five years! If my mother had still been alive, I would have been able to consult her regarding certain intimacies of the wedding night, but since that was not possible my Coop's past experiences got me through. I wondered as he had placed a folded towel under my hips last night, unaware of the physical changes which would be the result of our passion, saving me great embarrassment!

Not having had anything to eat since yesterday morning, I knew Coop must be famished! Bless his heart though; he had a hot bath prepared and ready for me in the room set aside for such niceties. I must admit that I enjoyed the relaxation of certain body parts as I submerged into that warm water. Knowing how hungry he must be, I didn't stay anywhere near as long as I would have liked….

After dressing, we started down the hall but paused at the top of the stairs. He turned and kissed me, looking once more with eyes so deep and blue that I almost lost myself in them. He smiled and looked back toward the room….

It wasn't until close to thirty minutes later that we made it downstairs to join Jessie and Vin, already half-way through their breakfast, smiling as though they had a secret that only they shared!

The Journal of Jessie Llewellyn

I have awakened very early this morning- the sun is just rising, and Vin is still asleep, curled up in the bed. I look at this wonderful man, dark curls tousled and drooping across his brow, those incredible blue eyes closed, and thank God I made the decision to go West- my "adventure" has contained so much light and so much darkness that it is almost impossible to believe I am the same woman who saw the sunrise through tears here in this town only a few months ago! I have found a sister, dearer to me than my own, and the one being with whom I hope to spend the rest of my life... God willing! I feel as if I were the sun, rising gently and lighting the world with joy, not only for myself, but for Mary and her husband and for my beloved Vin! I look at my ring, light and dark forever entwined, and think of this moment as my real birth- twenty-eight years late but here at last! He is stirring, reaching for me as I sit here

writing...

COOP

If anyone had ever told me years ago that I would feel the way I do right now, I would've laughed at them. Never in a million years could I have guessed how the right gal could make me feel so... happy... so loved... so... complete! It isn't just the physical release, hell, it certainly ain't like I never done the act before... it's more that... she gave everything that she is to me... It sure was worth waitin' for. Glad I had the good sense not to push her before, when she wasn't ready. Last night she gave herself to me freely. She was now mine. Mine in body, heart and spirit! I've never experienced a sensation like this... It's almost intoxicatin'.

MARY

Heading downstairs once more, breakfast on our minds, Coop asked, "Why are you blushin', darlin'?"

Stopping at the top of the stairs, "It's just that everyone will know what we've been doing," I whispered, suddenly shy.

He turned and took my hands. Smiling, "Sweetheart, most of those people don't even know us, or know that we were married just yesterday, so they have no idea. Heck, it probably won't even cross their minds to wonder about it... You know you don't need to worry about Jessie and Vin, as they know what happens with married couples."

"I know… It's just…"

"Just that we are husband and wife and anything we did last night is covered by that little piece of paper," he said, laughing. "Just walk in like nothin's changed, darlin' and no one will notice."

The Journal of Jessie Llewellyn

We were in the midst of breakfast in the hotel dining room when Mary and Coop walked in, Mary looking like sunrise herself, and Coop with a proud air which would have been funny, had it not been so obviously filled with love! It was a very happy quartet that lingered over breakfast this morning, even though we must attend a celebration that is most likely to resemble the funeral of a detested relative. At least we are all armed with last night's wonderful memories to sustain us.

VIN

When Coop and Mary walked into the dinin' room this mornin', they both looked like somebody'd left 'em a million dollars! Jessie was smilin' so big – she was just shinin' with happiness for her "sister" and seein' her look like that made me wanta grab her and run straight back up to her hotel room! That smile o' hers just lights the world up – for me, anyhow. I guess most folks don't have champagne for breakfast, but the waiter didn't turn a hair when I ordered a bottle… maybe he's used to weddin' breakfasts… Knowin' we had to go to that party at Jessie's folks made gettin' a little drunk even more enticin', I gotta admit. But we'd all survive it and then we'd be on our own....at last!

The Journal of Jessie Llewellyn

Thank fortune it is over, and we are back at the hotel. A funeral for a despised relation would have been slightly less amusing, but just as awkward. We arrived at Mama's and Papa's house at three pm- afternoon parties being the "accepted thing" for celebrating engagements in "our set," as Mama put it- not that I care any longer for the "accepted thing," but it does make sense. If family members bring their offspring, the smallest ones can be put to nap in one of the bedrooms with an older sibling in charge. The elder children are not yet cranky and obnoxious being up past their bedtime!

The children, amazingly, were the best thing about this celebration, as they swarmed Vin and Coop, both in "city suits" but of Western cut, for the affair. If they had intended to "blend in," they did not take into account the family "grapevine," which had already stirred the hearts of all the male junior cousins regarding my Vin. There was some consternation and confusion amongst the adults when they thought there were two Vin Harpers at the party, but those who had mistakenly decided that either Mary or I were interested in bigamy, found themselves denied such delicious fare for gossip! It is a tribute, I think, to the success of my efforts to convince the family that I am beyond redemption that they even entertained the notion!

Coop and Vin, bless them, did their best to be quintessential cowboys, which delighted the little boys, made the men pea green with envy, and fascinated the women. Our two gentlemen gallantly stepped forward to amuse, entertain, and baffle the company, so Mary and I were left fairly free of the usual feminine sniping that such affairs abound in- a much needed respite after four visits from my sisters in one week.

At least Papa was generous enough to provide champagne. The four of us definitely needed a little "medicinal" beverage to make it past the second hour of the festivities until we could gracefully excuse ourselves. Mary and Coop received many congratulations on their wedding, most accompanied by sly looks, as she revealed that they had wed just yesterday. It didn't bother them - both of them are floating on a rosy cloud where nothing but love lives - Bless them…

When we were finally able to escape, Mary and I, thanks to our warm coats, thoroughly enjoyed the brisk pace that Coop set with the buggy. We had been served many delicacies and a few substantial viands at the party, so Mary and I were not interested in dinner, but our "boys" were, as usual, more than ready for a meal! Vin suggested they repair to the nearest establishment that served both alcohol and food and celebrate the wedding, and Coop enthusiastically agreed, after giving Mary a questioning look. Vin looked at me, too, but only to share the novelty of Coop seeking approbation before going out for gentlemanly entertainment! I certainly did not mind - those two dear men had definitely earned it! Mary and I went up to what is now my room (and Vin's) to have a bit of good woman -to-woman talk, while our men headed out of the hotel to salute the nuptials in their own way.

MARY

While Coop and Vin were enjoying dinner and drinks and male camaraderie, Jessie and I retired to the room which we had shared up until last night. Sitting on the side of the bed I began, "I am so sorry if we put you and Vin in an awkward position last night."

Jessie smiled, "Honey, I'll be honest with you," she said patting my hand, "last night was not our first time together."

I know I just stared for a moment and then thought back to our time in Wyoming and all the "walks and rides" which they had taken. She smiled as the realization dawned on my face.

"He was my first and only and last night was wonderful and enjoyed, so do not feel as though you put us on a path of "illicit liaison," shall we say?"

"You don't know how relieved I am! I have to admit neither of us was thinking about much of anything except…. well…"

"Oh, we figured that pretty quickly!" she laughed.

We chatted a bit more about this and that then, having procrastinated long enough, I said, "Jessie, Coop and I have checked the train schedule and there's a train heading East tomorrow morning. If all goes well, we hope to reach Virginia in four days." I paused briefly, "Now that Coop is along, I won't need an escort and I know y'all would probably want some time together…. Of course, you're invited if you would rather join us!"

"No, dear, Vin will be returning to St. Joseph to begin his training with the Pinkerton's, and I believe it would be beneficial that I be there near Mr. Sutcliffe in the event my father attempts something nefarious!"

We enjoyed our "girl talk" until there was a quiet knock on the door and the boys entered.

"You ready to go home, darlin'?" Coop asked indicating our room across the hallway.

I joined him at the door and bade "good night" and farewell to these two wonderful people who were not only friends but also family.

The Journal of Jessie Llewellyn

Once Mary and Coop had retired to their room, Vin sat down in the easy chair and pulled me onto his lap, and, tipping my chin so I couldn't hide my eyes, said, "Little girl, are you envious of Mary?"

I must have looked like a startled owl- I could feel my eyes opening to their fullest extent, as I answered, "Envious? Why on earth would you think that, love?"

He looked into my eyes, and then looked at the ring on my left hand, held in his right, "Do you want us to get married right way? I saw what looked like a tear, when you hugged Mary this mornin'- I know you're happy for her an' all, but I worry that you might feel bad that we haven't tied the knot yet."

He looked so concerned and so unhappy that I just put my arms around him and kissed him as thoroughly as I knew how! Once I pulled back a little and could see his eyes, I said, "Vin, look at me."

He did, almost shyly, and I said, "Dearest love, if we never make it to the altar I won't care."

He looked astonished, but I could see he believed me. "Mi corazon, are you sure?"

"Of course, you foolish man! As far as I am concerned, we are as married as if we stood in the front of a cathedral full of people with three bishops officiating at our nuptials! Yes, I want us to be married in the eyes of the law, simply because I want to share everything I have with you, including my inheritance from Aunt Martha, but you told me once, when I was trying to "put my oar in" with Mary and Coop, that dangerous jobs make for hesitation when one has hostages to fortune! If I did anything to lessen your ability to do your job and survive, I would never forgive myself!"

He wrapped me in his arms again, and kissed the top of my head before replying, "Then, little girl, as soon as I've taken this job and found out just where I'll be, we'll find a justice of the peace and get the most important job done!"

"Vin, I will always want, need, and love you- if you are sure that I won't be a source of danger for you, then I'll run to the first JP we can find!" I said, trembling a little with the love I felt for this man. "One thing though, my love, " I said, "Mary would never forgive me if she wasn't there to see us married, so we need to wait at least until they get back from Virginia!"

"Virginia?" he said, questioningly.

"Oh, I forgot to tell you! You are a dangerous distraction, dearest, all by yourself! They are leaving in the morning for Mary's home. They hope to accomplish the trip in four days, but I don't know how long her family business will take. They plan to return to St. Joseph when it's concluded and then from there, head back to Wyoming. I need to see Mr. Sutcliffe in St. Joseph anyway- something Papa said has me a bit worried - so we can head back there tomorrow, and I will be with you!"

"Fine by me, little girl," said my Vin, "now that we have that settled, how about we turn in?"

"Just what I was thinking, love," I said and, with his able assistance, prepared to retire for the night.

MARY

We rose early and left for the train depot, Coop and I. We had made our goodbyes to Jessie and Vin last night. How I miss them already...

"I managed to get us a sleeper compartment. It should make the trip more comfortable and, uh, interestin'…," said Coop with a gleam in his eyes.

"James Cooper Martin!" I said with false chastisement. "What am I to do with you?"

Taking me up in an embrace, "I can think of a thing or two," he murmured into my ear.

Oh, my, but I am glad we are married, I thought, blushing at where my mind led me!

The Journal of Jessie Llewellyn

Vin and I paid an obligatory farewell call on Mama and Papa yesterday, before we left Alton for St. Joseph. I was a bit surprised to receive a warm hug and kiss from Mama- I believe that it was partly her relief that this "odd" daughter of hers was going to be well away from the family for a good long while, perhaps even permanently! I could be mistaken, but Mama always treated me like a hen who has accidentally acquired a falcon's egg to raise, and is both terrified and bewildered by its tendency to fly off with little or no warning!

Papa kissed me on the cheek and shook hands with Vin, giving us the conventional fatherly blessing and requesting news of our future plans. I wish that I had a closer relationship with my parents in some ways, but that would require drastic changes in either my character or theirs!

We have checked into the Prescott House in St. Joseph, a different hotel from that in which we stayed on our previous visit- it is comfortable and convenient to both the Pinkerton offices and Mr. Sutcliffe. We discussed on the train today whether or not to request two rooms- Vin would have gladly done so to "protect" my reputation, but it seemed foolish to me. Instead, we decided to register as Mr. & Mrs. Harper. It will most certainly be accurate in the very near future! I must remember to mention to the desk clerk that we are newlyweds and that I might receive messages or letters directed to my maiden name!

Vin will go to the Pinkerton's offices in the morning- once he has accepted a position with them, we will know better how to proceed. I plan to visit Mr. Sutcliffe either tomorrow or the next day- I am somewhat concerned about Papa's needing "aid" from him! I miss Mary and Coop, but I am most pleased that they will have a "wedding tour" of their own! It is a bit disconcerting to be temporarily in "limbo" regarding our future, but as long as mine is with Vin, nothing else matters!

MARY

Miss Jessie Llewellyn

c/o Mr. Jacob Sutcliffe, Esq

St. Joseph, Missouri

November 16, 1874

My Dear Jessie,

Coop and I arrived in Richmond yesterday evening. The city has rebuilt quite nicely from the devastation of several years ago, although I do not believe it will ever be as beautiful as I remember it from my childhood visits, but then, we notice such different things when we are young.

We shall be leaving shortly, as Coop is making arrangements for a private coach to take us to River's View. It would be quicker and more comfortable to travel down the James River to River's View, but I wanted the time to contemplate what I may find once we arrive there. I have not wired ahead, so no one knows that we are coming. As daddy used to say, 'Always keep them guessing' and so I shall! I hope my fears are unsubstantiated but only time will tell...

I will keep in touch as the days go by, but I fear any news will not be that interesting, although you might enjoy reading about a new frock more than did my Coop. Should you need to contact us the address is: Mr. and Mrs. James Cooper Martin, River's View, Charles City, Virginia. I appreciate your patience as I realize you know who we are, but I find such pleasure in writing out our names.

Silly, I know…

One bit of advice I would like to impart to you… however you can manage, you and Vin must take a train trip in a sleeping compartment. It was amazing! I shall leave the rest to your imagination…

My Sincerest Regards,

Mrs. James Cooper Martin

The Journal of Jessie Llewellyn

I knew I was right to be concerned about Papa! When I called on Mr. Sutcliffe today, Vin was not with me, perhaps fortunately! He had gone to the Pinkerton's offices to accept their offered position and knew that I would visit Aunt's lawyer- it was to be a brief call and both of us assumed that it would be a kind of "progress" report of any details of Aunt's estate. Vin knew I planned to inquire about Papa's mention of needing Mr. Sutcliffe's aid- now that I know just what that "aid" was to be I am quite glad that Papa is in Illinois and Vin and I are over three hundred miles away! Mr. Sutcliffe was most pleased to see me and assured me that all arrangements for the trust had been completed. He also told me that my share could be distributed to me in the form of a bank draft that would be honored in Laramie, as I had informed him that I would be returning there, although I did not know exactly when. I explained about Vin's offer from the Pinkerton agency and the difficulty of planning until we knew exactly what that would entail.

"My dear Miss Llewellyn, " he said, with a smile, "I am pleased for you and your fiancé! Pinkerton's has a most excellent reputation-as you know, I have engaged them myself in many matters and have never been disappointed in their expertise!"

He expressed some concern about the 'often dangerous' nature of their work, but when I told him that I was aware, he let the matter drop.

"Mr. Sutcliffe, if it will not violate your sense of honor or confidentiality, I would like to ask you something," I said.

Mr. Sutcliffe looked a bit startled, but said, "Of course, Miss Llewellyn. I will surely tell you if such a circumstance should arise!"

"My father said something about seeking your aid when we were visiting my family in Illinois," I began, "if it is possible, I would like to know if he has been in communication with you and just what assistance he requested."

To my surprise, Mr. Sutcliffe began to laugh heartily! I must have looked rather put out, as I had not intended to be amusing, so he apologized and said, "My dear girl- the matter with which he sought my assistance was so ridiculous that I couldn't help reliving my reaction to his letter! He asked me to initiate procedures to have you declared insane!"

VIN

I'd spent some time at the Pinkerton agency gettin' to know some of the men there and makin' sure that everythin' was straight regardin' my "reputation." Grantley was even friendlier that the last time I'd seen him and poured me a good whiskey form the bottle he kept in his desk.

"So, Vin," he said, "looks like you and the Pinkerton Agency are working together."

"Fine by me," I answered and took a sip of that fine whiskey, "What's on the cards now?"

"We'll need you to spend a few weeks here in St. Jo for trainin' purposes," Grantley said, smilin', "but you'll be on salary during that time."

"Sounds OK," I said, "but I'm not much for city life…."

"I can well understand that," he replied, pouring himself another drink. "We need men familiar with the West, Vin, and you fit that bill. Once you've gone through our training and gotten comfortable with some of the jobs we do, we'll be sending you West again, probably to Cheyenne or Denver."

"I'd rather Cheyenne," I said, "I've gotten familiar with Wyomin' and I like it…made some friends there, too."

"I'll take that into account," Grantley said, noddin' his head, "our man in Cheyenne has been asking for more agents based there – we're getting more and more jobs running security on the railroads…. lots of cash and gold being transferred to and from banks here in the east and too damned many outlaws interested in intercepting it."

"Ain't surprisin'," I remarked, thinkin' of our little adventure on the way to St. Jo.

"Smithers will be delighted," Grantley said, offerin' to top off my half empty glass.

I shook my head – and he smiled, like I'd done somethin' that pleased him. Knowin' enough about Pinkerton, I wasn't about to

seem like a hard drinkin' man – workin' for an agency that had access to information about gold shipments meant bein' right careful about over indugin'. Much as I'd have liked another – that was mighty good whiskey – I wasn't about to make him think I'd be a liability due to drink! We talked a bit more and then said goodbye. I decided to go on back to the hotel and wait for Jessie – she'd gone to the law office and I was expectin' her back early, since it was mostly just checkin' in with Mr. Sutcliffe. I picked up a newspaper on the way back to the hotel and figgered to do some readin' in case she
hadn't got back there yet.

MARY

"So, tell me more about this plantation of yours, darlin'," said Coop as we were en route.

"It was originally a small home built around 1745 by great-great grandfather, Owen McDonnaugh. He had been a sea Captain and chose the spot because the James is still navigable all the way up to Richmond and River's View formed a natural little cove. It's been passed down through the generations and added on to as time went by." Shaking my head, "I never thought it would come to me! Firstly because of my gender and secondly because I had four older brothers! Two succumbed to fever before their teens and the other two were lost to us during the Conflict. Then when my parents died in the coach accident… well, it just seemed like the gentleman suitors were only after my property."

He reached over and took my hand in his, cradling it against his chest, "I'm sorry, darlin'."

It still amazes me how kind and gentle yet strong and wild this man of mine is! "I just wish Mama and Daddy could have met you and know that I am in safe hands and loved!"

As our carriage turned onto the property, the workers in the fields looked up at our progress. I thought I recognized one of them and waved, "Annie!" I called.

"Miz. Mary! I'll be! It's Miz. Mary!" she hollered to the others. With that, several of the workers ran to the carriage to greet us. I had the driver stop as they approached.

"Glory be! It's a blessed day!" cried Annie. "Do Mista Evans know you a'comin?" she asked.

"No, not yet!" I smiled.

"Good!"

This caught my attention as Annie had always been a faithful attendant, judicious worker and, since my childhood, a friend. "What's this about Annie?"

She looked to the others standing around us. They all dipped their heads, but she returned her gaze to mine, "Things have been changin' since you been gone Missy..."

Realizing she didn't want to say more right then, I introduced my Coop, to whom they all expressed their joy, and I thanked them all for the welcome.

Before we could proceed, I heard a hard, mean voice, "Get back to work! Now!"

They dispersed and returned to the field as the man approached. He tipped his hat to me, "Beggin' your pardon, but can I help y'all?"

"We have come to see Mr. Evans," I replied.

"Yes, ma'am, you'll be wantin' to go straight to the house there," he directed. "Drive on!"

Looking over at me with concern my Coop asked, "Are you all right?" I nodded. "I take it that wasn't what you were anticipatin'?"

"No," I responded grimly. "Something is very wrong."

Alighting from the carriage, with Coop's assistance, I walked straight into the house without knocking or waiting for admittance.

A man came in from the parlor with one eyebrow raised and addressed me in a somewhat huffy manner, "May I help you, madam, sir?" he said as he surveyed me and then Coop.

Not missing a beat, I replied, "Yes. Please take our bags to my room and have someone run a bath as I wish to remove the dust from my trip." When he just stood there looking as though I had grown two heads before his very eyes, I continued, waving my hand and dismissing him, "Go along now, that will be all!"

Astonishment on his face, he stammered, but I ignored him and indicated to Coop that he should follow me into the parlor. "Oh, and please have someone bring some tea in for me and my husband as we are parched from our travels!"

Obviously, he was not a butler, although I treated him that way, intentionally, but he went to find someone to do my bidding.

A look of awe on his face, my Coop shook his head and whispered, "Who are you?"

I only smiled. "A girl has to have some surprises," I said, relinquishing a kiss to my husband.

It didn't take long before my cousin entered with the man we had met earlier. "May I help you?" she said and then gasped as I turned to face her.

"Hello, Jeanette."

"Mary! How… nice to have you visit..."

"Visit…? Hmmm, perhaps..."

"You're planning on staying a while?"

Cutting a quick glance at Coop I replied, "Oh, dear me, let me introduce you to my husband, James Cooper Martin, of the Martin's of Galveston. He and I might just move back in."

I was rewarded with looks of panic from Jeanette and the man I would later discover was her fiancé.

"Would you please arrange for Josiah to give my husband a tour of our home? Oh, and I wish to meet with your parents, after my bath, of course." Then in dismissal, "Thank you."

Jeanette had the good grace to leave us, taking the man with her.

An hour later, after changing out of my traveling clothes and refreshing myself in the bath, I donned a comfortable although stylish dress and prepared myself to meet with my Aunt Lydia, who was my mothers' sister, and her husband, Frank Evans. Their home had been on the outskirts of Richmond and had been one of the buildings razed to the ground as the Union army passed through. They had moved into town where Frank had been a banker, until I had offered them positions to manage River's View in my absence.

As I entered the parlor, Uncle Frank rose, and Aunt Lydia greeted me. "Niece, whyever have you returned so soon?"

"So soon? Why, I have been away for almost six months!"

"My, how time flies," muttered Frank.

At that moment, Coop returned from his tour of the grounds and joined us. I introduced him to looks of surprise from my aunt and uncle.

"I just thought I'd let y'all know that there will be a meeting tomorrow with my attorneys. I sent notice to them when we were in Richmond. They should arrive just after noon and partake of luncheon. Afterwards we will discuss what will become of River's View." This was met with alarmed glances from my relatives. "Now, if you please, my husband and I would like some time alone. We will see y'all at dinner." Thus, they were, for lack of any better description, dismissed.

"Somethin' I need to know about, darlin'?"

I smiled and replied, "I have been in touch with my lawyers these past months and have received some troubling news. The ledger reports from Uncle Frank and what I have received from my lawyers do not calculate out the same. I've been over them dozens of times, hence my journey here." I sighed and added, "I may have to turn Aunt Lydia and her family out…."

He enfolded me in an embrace. "Well, darlin', I sure don't envy your decision, but I'll support whatever you think is best."

"I'm sorry I haven't filled you in more about what I thought might be going on. I guess I didn't want to believe it but coming here and seeing things for myself has made me realize that something must change. This is not how my Daddy ran the place." I began to pace, "Those workers out there reminded me more of slave labor than what they were under my fathe'rs supervision and I'll not revert to the ways of his parents! He worked too hard to set them up with abodes for the families and education for them, so they could read, write and cypher. Under his plan they could either go free after their time here to repay the price daddy put forth for their purchase, or they could stay on for wages."

"Your father actually allowed them to leave once their purchase price was paid?"

"Yes. There is a large settlement of free blacks just outside of Williamsburg." I crossed to Coop and continued, "Daddy was an adherent of Thomas Jefferson's writings, you see. Mr. Jefferson had laid out a plan to free his slaves and had succeeded with some but not the majority, unfortunately. He believed that were the slaves not trained or educated, they would starve or be forced into lives of crime, and since they were his responsibility, he couldn't free them all! But we had the fortune to do just that and the workers you saw as we came home are all free men and women and here by choice, I am proud to say. Come hell or high water, I am going to get to the bottom of this!"

My sweet Coop just released a deep breath and joined me by the window, "You're kinda a force of nature when you get your dander up," he said, ever the one for understatement.

I turned in wonder and thought how blessed I was to have him in my life.

COOP

I had only caught watery glimpses of this side of Mary over the past several months... now I wondered just who I have married…

The look on the faces of her relatives was worth the whole trip! I got a bad feelin' somethin' was goin' on here. At least Mary seems to be prepared for that possibility. She's definitely a force to be reckoned with and I'm willin' to be swept up in whatever comes our way, standin' beside her to help however I may… to protect her with my very life if the need should arise.

MARY

Following a rather strained dinner, my family made themselves scarce, so Coop and I retired to the parlor. The windows were open to the chilly evening air, a breeze moving in off the James.

"Dearest, would you join me on a stroll?" I asked.

Gallantly he complied, placing my shawl across my shoulders and taking my elbow.

As we moved away from the house, I said conspiratorially, "I must get down to Annie's home and see what more she has to say regarding what's going on!"

At Annie's, her husband opened the door in reply to my knock. "Oh, Edward! How good to see you!"

"Ma'am," he replied.

"Ma'am?" I questioned as I have known both Annie and Edward since I was a small child!

He smiled, "Miz Mary…"

I supposed I would have to be happy with that and introduced my Coop to them. They both made a big to-do over him and I believe he even blushed.

Edward showed us to some stools and Annie set down some good ole homemade pie. "Do you like pie, Mr. Martin?" asked Annie.

I had to laugh at that, knowing the answer.

"Yes, ma'am, I do!" replied my beloved.

Following the pleasantries, I asked them to tell me more about what had been happening since my departure. The stories they told me made my blood run hot. I only realized that I was shaking when Coop put his hand over mine. So distraught was I at how my home was being mismanaged, I felt on the verge of tears! I had thought of selling River's View or even letting my aunt and uncle manage it for me, but neither option appeared possible now. I would not let my workers be mistreated as they were, and my good family name violated!

It wasn't overly late by the time Coop and I returned to the house, but most of the lights in the living quarters were already out, which seemed odd.... We were tired after the long day and retreated to my room. Our room...

The Journal of Jessie Llewellyn

When I returned to the hotel, Vin was in our room reading the newspaper. As I came in, he looked up and something in my face must have given him pause, because he immediately came to me and put his arms around me, giving me a long and thorough kiss!

In spite of my agitation, I found myself melting into his arms as if

87

we two were the only beings in the wide universe! Finally, when we both drew breath, I managed to say, "You, my beloved, are the best man in the world!"

"He smiled at me and quirked that eyebrow, saying, "Little girl, you must have had quite a day. I appreciate the compliment, but I don't think I qualify for that position!"

"Oh, love" I said, "I think you have been able to divert my thoughts enough to avoid my committing patricide!!"

"Whoa, mi corazon - I'm no scholar but does that mean what I think it does? You plannin' on murderin' your papa? What did that lawyer fella say to you?" Vin led me to the chair, sat down, and pulled me onto his lap.

I leaned against his shoulder, so very thankful to feel him holding me close, and muttered, "I wish I could murder him, love- that ..."

Words failed me (something that does not often happen, but I couldn't think of anything vile enough to use to describe Papa's request). "OK, honey, tell me about it- I'm here, you're here, and he's off in Illinois, so whatever he's done we can't do anything about it right at this moment!"

"Vin, he wrote to Mr. Sutcliffe to ask him to take steps to have me declared insane!"

For a moment I didn't think he'd heard me- he was so still and quiet that I raised my eyes to see if he was paying attention and I saw a Vin I had never seen before. He looked as if he were carved from wood, only his eyes alive -those beautiful eyes that usually sparkled with love when he looked at me were chips of blue ice! I remembered Coop describing what Vin had looked like after he shot my despicable cousin and I finally understood his meaning. I wasn't afraid, but I was amazed at the change! "This is the man I love with all my heart," I thought, "God forbid that my anger should drive him to do something that we both would regret!"

I reached up and touched his cheek, and he looked at me, eyes warming, but still as rigid as stone. "Vin," I said, "It's all right, truly! I am very angry at Papa for this, but he cannot do such a thing. Mr. Sutcliffe told me, after I had recovered a bit from the shock of hearing this, that he wrote back to Papa and said that I was the sanest person he knew, and that if Papa tried anything of the sort, Mr. Sutcliffe would personally initiate a lawsuit against him for defamation of character and attempted larceny."

Vin relaxed slightly, and said, "At least Mr. Sutcliffe has a brain in his head!"

"I'm sorry, love," I said, "for blurting it out that way, but I was just so angry and hurt that I couldn't help it!"

"It's all right, little girl," he said, returning to the Vin I knew, "It's a damned good thing, though, that your daddy is out of my reach right now! I'd hate to have you take our wedding tour by yourself 'cause I was in jail."

"Believe me, beloved, I am most grateful for that as well," I said, smiling into his once again sparkling eyes, "otherwise we'd both be in jail!"

He laughed and held me close and I knew, once the hurt had eased a bit, that I would be able to laugh at the absurdity of it, just as Mr. Sutcliffe had. "You know, love," I said, "I must be really good at acting- perhaps I should consider a career on the stage!"

"How come?" he asked, looking at me a bit suspiciously. "I must have done a magnificent job convincing my sisters that I was as crazy as a basketful of bedbugs for Papa to think he had a chance in Hades of getting Aunt's estate that way!" Vin laughed so hard that I fell off his lap! His solicitous care of my poor damaged self that night was well worth the fall!

MARY

The next morning found us still abed at the late hour of eight a.m.! It was chilly this morning; frost was rimed on the windows. We rose and dressed quickly. When we went downstairs, there was no one else there except for the cook and houseman. Very strange...

"Where is the rest of the family?" I asked Linda, our cook, who had been here since before my eldest brother had been born.

"Miz. Mary, they left early this mornin'! I was jes' gettin' the wood for the stove and saw dem leavin'! They had baggage and everythin'!"

A look of alarm crossed Coop's face. "Do you think they're makin' a run for it?"

Nodding, "Yes, I do."

"Oh, Lordy, Miz. Mary! What if they go an' take all yo' money from the bank?" cried Linda.

Coop looked startled at that prospect. "You don't think there's any chance of that, do you?"

I took his hand this time and smiled, "Let them try," I purred.

Both eyebrows had risen up under his hair.

"I set a little trap in case that's what they intend!"

Shortly before noon, I received a letter from my attorneys in Richmond, sent via a dispatch rider.

I glanced at Coop as I opened the letter, my hands shaking.

Dear Mrs. Martin,

We regret to inform you that your plan was put to the test but implemented successfully. We have your aunt, uncle, niece and her fiancé in jail as they attempted to remove all the money from your accounts.

We will be detained from our appointment with you and your husband until tomorrow, mid-afternoon. We beg your forgiveness for our tardiness but as it is to take care of your interests, we are certain you will understand.

Kind Regards,

M. Miller, Esq.

T. Rose, Esq.

I passed the letter to Coop after I finished it. Looking up he shook his head. Wonderingly he asked, "How did you know?"

"I didn't. I hoped it was all just a big mistake, but I had to take precautions. I am just glad that my mother wasn't alive to witness her sister's deception."

"Well, I'm glad to discover the gal I married is not only beautiful but smart to boot," he said as he lifted me and held me close.

COOP

Mary tried her best to hide her disappointment in her aunt. I know it cut her deep when the need for her plan to be implemented became necessary. I knew she was hurtin' inside. Takin' her in my arms, I held her as she trembled in the aftermath of the day.

To think, she had taken on this burden to herself…

After a bit, I pulled away far enough to look into her eyes. "You know, darlin', you don't have to do these things all on your own. I'm here to help… to share… to support you…"

She raised a hand to my face. "I've had to rely upon my own decisions and choices for so long… It will be difficult to learn to share these things."

"It's what couples do." I took her hands in mine. "You trust me, don't you?"

"With all my heart."

"Then from now on, we act as one. Agreed?"

"Agreed," she said, sealing her answer with a kiss.

The Journal of Jessie Llewellyn

The past few days have been peaceful - a nice change after my discovery of Papa's perfidy! Vin has been assured by the Pinkerton Agency that, although he will need to remain in St. Joseph for another two or three weeks, he will eventually be based in the Cheyenne offices - wonderful news, as I do so long to return to Wyoming! Had it been otherwise, I would, of course, go wherever Vin was to be- I would not be comfortable or happy too far from my source of light in darkness, and his tender love!

I have received a letter from Mary- it was posted in Richmond, Virginia, and she has given me her address at her property in Charles

City. I believe I shall follow her advice about train travel as soon as possible- on our return West, I hope! I am sure she has arrived at her home by now, as her letter was dated several days ago. I don't know whether I should write her about Papa's little scheme- I am still quite angry at him, and even though Vin probably has decided not to shoot Papa, I'm not so sure that either Coop or Mary might not decide to visit Alton on their way West and perform that office for us! I am going to ask her to stand up with us when they return to St. Joseph- I know Vin wants Coop to do so, also, so I will get a letter off in the post today.

Mr. & Mrs. James Cooper Martin

River's View

Charles City, Virginia

November 20, 1874

Dearest Mary and Coop,

I am so glad that both of you enjoyed your train travel. I shall take your recommendation, Mary, regarding our travel arrangements when we return to Wyoming. Vin has accepted the position with the Pinkerton's, so we will be here in St Joseph for about two weeks. It looks as if he will be based in Cheyenne after that, thus Wyoming will see us again very soon.

I have a favor to ask of both of you: Vin and I plan to marry here in St. Joseph before he takes up the posting in Cheyenne. Would you stand up with us at our marriage? Having you both with us will make it even more special and quite delightful! I have other news that will wait until I see you- don't worry it is not another robbery or disaster! I hope all is well at River's View and that you two are enjoying the beginnings of married life! Feel free to write me c/o Mr. Sutcliffe, who is most assiduous in protecting my interests!

Much love,

Jessie Llewellyn (soon to be Mrs. Vin Harper!)

COOP

I was pleased that, as we waited for the arrival of Mary's attorneys, she filled me in on her plans. It seems our little discussion of yesterday was taken to heart. It felt good to know that she trusted me and took me into her confidence… as it should be with husband and wife. I suppose we are both still learnin' as we go along on this adventure called marriage.

"What do you think, dearest?" she asked.

"I think that if you believe this is the route to take, then I am in all the way."

She smiled and placed a small hand on my chest. "Thank you, my husband."

Smilin' back, I replied, "You're welcome, my wife."

When she giggled at that, I thought it was the most beautiful sound I'd ever heard…

MARY

It wasn't until three in the afternoon that the attorneys arrived, as it is approximately a five-hour journey horseback from their office in Richmond to River's View. I discussed my plans with them, which received some raised eyebrows from the pair. "If you are certain, Mrs. Martin, that this is how you wish to proceed, we will, of course, create the most beneficial plan for you."

I dispatched Reginald, an elderly man who had been with us since my grandfather's time and who now acted as butler to the family, to bring Edward and Annie. .He was also to bring the "Overseer," for that is how I thought of him after witnessing the mistreatment of the workers yesterday! As we waited on their arrivals, Linda presented our guests with tea and small cakes and such for their repast.

Once all were gathered, I began immediately with the "Overseer." "My attorneys have drawn a cheque for your services and two week's severance. Your presence here is no longer required. Good day."

He sat there a moment, digesting what he had heard, before leaping from the chair, turning a brilliant shade of red and had begun spewing forth profanities! It was as though lightening had struck as my Coop was there, placing himself between me and the creature. I cannot say that he ushered him out, it was more that my husband picked him up bodily and threw him onto the front porch, leaving the workers to "escort" him from the property which they did with pleasure!

"Thank you, my love," I said, laying a hand on his arm as he returned to the parlor. I hoped he knew from the look in my eyes just how grateful I was and how fortunate I felt that he was mine.

Then I turned back to the task at hand. "Edward, Annie, I suppose you are curious as to why you are here..." They nodded, not trusting their voices and still looking at Coop with a trace of awe. "I have known the both of you since I was a little girl. I know what kind of people y'all are. So here is the proposition...."

They looked at each other. "Edward, my father always said that you had a natural ability with the farming of the land and the people who worked it. I must agree, and I apologize for my relatives demoting you from the position you held. I want to rectify this and employ you as my Foreman." When he looked as though he had reservations, I continued, "You can read, write, and I'll wager, cypher better than that man we just terminated. The workers know and respect you, and in my mind, there is no one else better for the job."

Looking unsure, he turned to Annie who took his hand and smiled with pride. "I would be honored Miz. Ma-, uh, Mrs. Martin!"

"Wonderful!" Next, I turned my attention upon Annie. "I will need someone to run River's View for me in my absence, so I ask that you take on the post of Head Woman." Her eyes wide, I continued, "Before you say "no," let me assure you that I will cover all you will need to know to run that aspect of the plantation. You have already done this in a lesser degree for years dealing with the needs of the other workers. I have confidence in your abilities." Still seeing resignation at the thought of the tasks before them, I continued, "Rest assured that I will answer any questions you have expeditiously, and Mr. Miller and Mr. Rose are just up in Richmond and will offer their guidance as well!" I could see a hundred things running through her mind as I took her hands, "Yes?"

Looking to Edward and then back at me, "Yes!"

"Good! I am certain y'all are up to the challenge. Of course, it would mean that y'all would need to move into the main house." As a protest began to form, "You both know that a house unlived-in deteriorates rapidly. We need to know that there is someone looking out for our interests who will love and cherish our home and treat it as we would, if we are to return to the West, for that is our plan." As they tried to digest everything which had occurred to this moment, I added, "Oh, one more thing, there is a salary which befits the positions.'

Looking greatly overwhelmed and as though they may back away from the challenges, Coop stepped forward and put out his hand, "Well?"

Exchanging glances once more between them, Edward reached out to clasp Coop's hand, "Yes sir!"

The deal had been struck!

Mr. Rose spoke, "We will draw up the terms, Mrs. Martin."

"Thank you, sir. Your rooms have been made ready for your overnight stay. Dinner will be served in a couple hours. Please make yourselves comfortable."

The Journal of Jessie Llewellyn

Mr. & Mrs. Cooper Martin

River's View

Charles City, Virginia

November 22, 1874

My Dearest Mary & Coop,

I received a letter from Papa this week- more entreaties to reverse my decisions about Aunt's estate, scolding upon my choice to marry a "common laborer," and various dire predictions regarding my future in an "untamed and uncivilized wilderness!" This is much less annoying than his previous communications with Mr. Sutcliffe (about which I will inform you when you both return to St. Joseph!), so after wading through it, I promptly deposited it in the nearest waste basket!

I have refreshed my wardrobe with additional frocks for city life at minimal expense, as I have no desire to frequent the interminably boring "social events" of the city! Vin and I have attended one or two entertainments at the Tootle Opera House- a theater built to "rival those in New York," I heard one patron say. Vin has been engaged most days with his work at Pinkerton's- I believe that his expertise and knowledge of the Western "bad citizens" is deemed a boon to the Agency!

I look forward to hearing from you, dear friends, not only for yourselves, but for information on your expected return. I am so excited about having you both here for our wedding! It will likely be similar to your own, as the last thing I want for my wedding is an influx of my relatives. The sooner a thousand miles between my family and Mr. and Mrs. Harper, the happier I shall be!

With much love for you both,

Jessie Llewellyn

MARY

Miss Jessie Llewellyn

St. Joseph, Missouri

c/o Mr. Sutcliffe, Esq

November 23, 1874

Leaving Richmond this morning stop

See you in four days stop

M and C stop

The Journal of Jessie Llewellyn

Vin and I decided to visit Mr. Sutcliffe's office this morning to inform him of our plans. We had just been seated in his private office when in walked Mary and Coop! Mary and I exchanged rapturous hugs and our "boys" indulged in some handshakes and back slapping, so glad were we to be together again.

Mr. Sutcliffe was most indulgent of our displays of rejoicing and offered to take us to luncheon. Vin and I were astonished that the Martins had gotten into St Joseph so early, but Mary explained that they had traveled all night in a compartment in order to arrive a bit sooner than we expected- she grinned widely as she explained it. Vin, grinning, said, "I thank you kindly sir, but Miss Llewellyn and I have urgent business to attend to!"

Coop looked at him questioningly and remarked, "I was goin' to treat you two to lunch- Mary and I haven't had a bite since last night and I'm near famished."

Vin said, laughing, "Well, cousin, your belly'll just have to stay empty for a bit longer- you and your lovely wife are goin' to witness our weddin' - there's a Justice o' the Peace in this buildin' and that's where we're goin' - right now!"

He swept us all out the door so quickly that poor Mr. Sutcliffe had to shout, "Congratulations!" as we descended the stairs, Coop asking Vin, plaintively, "Why're you in such an all-fired hurry?!"

MARY

The Justice of the Peace was a squat fellow but with a very

dignified attitude. He seemed to relish that aspect of his job that united a couple in the "bonds of holy matrimony." He began to pontificate on the righteousness of marriage, etc, etc, until Vin looked down at him with a bit of a glare. Coop employed that "hurry up" hand gesture again, and the man decided to pick up the pace somewhat. Jessie and I were trying to maintain some shred of composure.

She looked radiant as Vin took her hands into his own. If I didn't know better, I would've said his hands were trembling slightly as he placed the ring upon her finger!

They did allow the officiate to say *all* the words for the ceremony unlike others who shall remain nameless… and when it was announced that he could kiss his bride Vin did so thoroughly and passionately.

As the signatures were affixed to the Certificate, Coop suggested we check into the hotel, and then we would help them celebrate by treating them to lunch. His words were punctuated by a loud growl from his stomach!

"I seem to recall there are dinin' cars on trains nowadays. Didn't y'all eat on that trip?" Vin asked, a gleam in his eyes.

I believe I may have blushed at the remark, and Coop experienced a coughing spate, Vin clapping him on his back a time or two.

Jessie moved close to Vin and, with a sparkle in her eyes she laughed, "Come, my dearest, take a little pity on them!"

The Journal of Jessie Llewellyn Harper

I have had the most beautiful wedding in the world! Mary and

Coop stood up with us at the Justice of the Peace's office, and we repaired to a photographer's establishment to have wedding pictures made. Unbeknownst to them, Vin and I arranged to have two pictures of the four or us hand-tinted- a belated wedding gift to Mary and Coop and a "family treasure" for Vin and me. We also had pictures made of each couple- so much fun, although I am sure no mere photograph could capture the happiness we all radiated! The photographer said that it would take a few days to finish the pictures, so Vin will bring the finished products with him when he joins us in Laramie, as Mary, Coop, and I will take the train West tomorrow. I wish that my darling husband were to be with us- I had planned to get a compartment for the two of us, as Mary highly recommended it for newlyweds!

At any rate, we are all going out this afternoon- Coop insisted that a celebration is in order immediately (the poor man is half-starved, it seems) so dinner will be an early one. and I'm sure there will be better champagne than Papa provided. I have dropped a letter in the post for Mr. Sutcliffe, advising him of our marriage and plans to depart - also that Vin would be in St. Joseph a few more days before leaving to join us. The Pinkerton's have some additional work for him here that will, hopefully, only take a few days to accomplish, and then my beloved will join me! In a sense, we have been "married" for quite a while, but now the hotel register is both legally and emotionally correct!

MARY

What a perfect ceremony! My friends are bound officially in matrimony. Jessie made the most beautiful bride and her Vin struck a handsome countenance. Looking at them, I am certain they will have as happy a life together as Coop and I.

They took pity on my poor Coop, whose stomach grumbled and murmured almost constantly throughout the wedding ceremony, almost as punctuation to the vows Jessie and Vin exchanged. Several times the Justice of the Peace paused, albeit briefly, sighing, at the melodious rumblings emitted by Coop's stomach. It was with great pleasure that we celebrated together over a meal following their wedding.

If I could change one thing, it would be that we did not have to leave for Laramie so soon, so Jessie and Vin could have more time together.

The Journal of Jessie Llewellyn Harper

Last night Vin carried me over the threshold of our hotel room- I was so vividly reminded of my half- dreaming, half-awake state as he carried me to his horse when we left that horrible cave! He is truly the glorious light in my darkness, and if our just passed night together is any indication, I am his! It was so terribly hard to say goodbye this morning- even though the motion of the train is not conducive to writing, I must confide to my journal my feelings- it will help me to keep from bursting into foolish tears. He held me as if he would never let go and I didn't want him to! I shall carry the memory of the passionate kiss I received all the way to Laramie, in hopes that it will be repeated as soon as possible!

My Vin whispered in my ear, as he assisted me to board the train, "Never forget- te amo, mi corazon!"

I turned before entering the car to see him one more time …. he looked so forlorn that I nearly jumped off the train into his arms!

Mary and I have had a chance to catch up on our various bits of news. It is remarkable how alike Vin and Coop are in some ways, even above their astonishing physical resemblance- Coop does the same perambulations on a train as my Vin. Even that resemblance is threatening to bring me to tears- I must stop being a watering pot and contrive to enjoy their company and our journey together.

MARY

Coop and I said our "goodbyes" to Vin, and left Jessie and him, so they could have some time to themselves. It wasn't until the Conductor indicated that all should board that she came to join us. We saved a seat by the window across from ours, so she could see Vin for as long as possible as the train pulled away from the station.

Jessie attempted to enter her thoughts into her journal while Coop and I played with a deck of cards he had purchased, until a cart was brought around with coffee and small sweets and savories, just the right size for a pleasant nibble. He kept looking around and stretching his neck and back, so I suggested he take a bit of a stroll.

"You ladies wouldn't mind?"

"No, dearest, just don't fall off!" I said with a giggle.

He smiled, stood and stretched mightily and then went for a walk between cabins to find something more interesting than two chatty females, although he was both gracious and smart enough not to say so!

Talk we did! We spoke of everything from River's View to

Jessie's father to outfits we had each purchased... I love my Coop, but it was so good to have Jessie to talk with again. My sister by choice and now my relative by marriage!

COOP

I'm glad Mary didn't mind me walkin' around a bit... Two cars down, there was a poker game goin' on. After a few hands, one of the players shook his head and rose, sayin' he couldn't afford to lose any more money, or his wife would change the locks to the house and not let him in! Lookin' around at those of us standin' there watchin', one of the players asked if any of us were interested in fillin' the vacant spot. Two and a half hours later, even though I'd been winnin' fairly regular, I gathered my take and thanked the other players as I rose to leave.

The man to my right said, "Don't you think we should have a chance to win some of our money back? After all, we ain't goin' nowhere!"

That brought a spate of laughter from everyone within earshot as we were on a movin' train!

"Well, gentlemen, I'm sure you'll all understand when I say that I am still a newlywed and my wife is waitin' for me in another car..."

Those seemed to be the magic words as there was some guffawin' and back slappin' involved, but I was allowed to depart without further complaints!

MARY

As much as we were enjoying catching up with all that had transpired while we were separated, I began to wonder where my husband had gotten off to.

Jessie seemed to divine my thoughts as she said, "Don't worry, honey, there aren't many places Coop could get to on a moving train!"

Smiling sheepishly, I said, "I suppose you're right… I just wonder what he could have found to keep him away for so long…"

"You won't have to wonder any longer," Jessie said, as she nodded her head in the direction behind me.

Turning to look, I saw my Coop heading our way, a triumphant grin on his face. He resumed his seat beside me just as we pulled into our stop for the night.

The Journal of Jessie Llewellyn Harper

To: Vin Harper c/o Pinkerton Agency

St Joseph, Missouri

November 29, 1874

Coop arrested Adamsville Nebraska STOP Mistaken identity STOP Need your help now STOP

MMM & JLH

MARY

I was becoming exasperated! The moron, who was sheriff of this town, was also an imbecile to boot!

"How many times do I have to tell you, this-is-not-Jess-Cooper!"

"Yes, ma'am, I hear ya! But the description fits, and he is worth $5,000 and I plan on collectin' it!"

I threw my hands up in the air in frustration, "You've seen his identification! His name is James Cooper Martin and he is my husband!'"

"Yes, ma'am, but those things can be falsified. And you can't produce the Marriage Certificate," he drawled.

"Be-cause-it-is-in-the-ship-ment-from-Vir-gin-i-a-to-La-ra-mie!" I stated as though speaking with a fool!

"Ahem. Darlin', send a telegram to Vin," said my beloved from the cell in which he was incarcerated.

"Quiet you!" said the idiot sheriff as he slammed shut the door between the cells and his office.

"I want to stay with my husband!" I shouted, almost on the verge of tears.

"Can't be doin' that, ma'am. I'm headin' home for the night, so you can't stay."

"What about him?" I pointed towards the back and Coop's cell. "You're just going to leave him here, alone? What if the building caught fire?!" I felt myself on the verge of hysteria.

"I'll be fine, darlin'," was my Coop's muffled reply. "Jessie, take care of her."

Jessie took me by the shoulders and whispered in my ear. "We had better get to the telegraph office before they close."

As I was being led out the door I yelled, "I'll be back tomorrow morning! He'd better be safe or believe me, there will be Hell to pay! Mark my words!"

COOP

After the sheriff had ushered Mary and Jessie out of his office, he poked his head in the back where I was. Movin' the water barrel just outside my cell he said, laughin', "That wife of yours sure is feisty, ain't she?"

"Let's just say she has certain ideas of how things should be, and we'll leave it at that."

"I'll be back with your dinner and then lock you in for the night."

Now that Mary and Jessie and the sheriff have gone, I could smile safely at my wife's irate response to the Sheriff. I hate that she's all upset, but it should be pretty interestin' to see what's gonna occur over the next couple of days... that oaf has no idea what he's in for!

The Journal of Jessie Llewellyn Harper

This is the most frustrating situation!!! No sooner had we disembarked from the train in Adamsville (where we had decided to spend the night) and found a cafe in which to have dinner, when a grossly overweight man with a star on his vest accosted us, pistol aimed at poor Coop, and rumbled, "Stand up, Cooper, and raise your hands as high as they can go!"

Startled, Mary and I looked at Coop, who was slowly rising from his chair, hands in the demanded position- there are no words to describe our feelings! This horrid individual snatched away Coop's gun, then marched our Coop, who was trying to disabuse this creature of his mistake, with Mary and me trailing after them, to the town's jail! He then proceeded to lock him in a cell! If Mary had had easy access to her pistol, I believe she would have shot this idiot and I wouldn't have blamed her in the least!!!!

Coop was amazingly calm and told her to telegraph Vin - smart man, Coop- but Mary tried again to get the sheriff (I assume that is what he is, but since he didn't bother to inform us of anything except his conviction that Coop was Jess Cooper, he could be anybody) to listen to her. Seeing she was making absolutely no headway and expecting her to pick up something heavy at any moment and hit him with it, I urged Mary to come with me, in hopes that we could get a wire off to Vin immediately, but the telegraph office was closed.

Now we must wait until morning to telegraph. We do not even have the photographs taken at our wedding to confirm our identities, thanks to the absurd length of time it takes to process them. We have found lodging in a rooming house, though both of us are unlikely to sleep much tonight. Apparently, this buffoon has an old wanted circular accusing Jess Cooper of murder in some town in Colorado Territory and, as the cousins resemble each other so closely, the picture looks very much like Coop! This greedy excuse for a law officer is avid for the $5,000 reward listed on the circular and quite disinclined to listen to reason! I hope, once we have wired to Vin, that he will come as soon as possible to our aid!

After an almost sleepless night, Mary and I managed to dress ourselves and go to the cafe for coffee- neither of us was hungry, so after a restorative cup and some discussion of our perilous situation, I headed for the telegraph office and Mary went to the jail to see her poor husband. I wired Vin as economically and succinctly as I could with little sleep and a great deal of anger and worry. I then went to the jail to see Coop and let him know that I had successfully sent for help.

The idiot with the badge had at least allowed Mary to see her husband, although he watched them suspiciously at all times. I sat down in the one available chair (dusty enough to have been exhumed from an ancient tomb in Egypt!!) and thought about how much I wanted my Vin and the trouble he was facing when he did arrive! Surely, with his Pinkerton credentials and his resemblance to Coop, the idiot could be made to see reason!!!

MARY

Sitting adjacent to the jail cell, which my Coop occupied, we held hands through the bars. I told him that Jessie was sending a telegram off to Vin. Hopefully everything would get cleared up once his cousin arrived.

"My dear, sweet Coop," I said, patting his hands, "I am so sorry you have to go through this."

"It ain't no big thing darlin', as long as you're alright."

"No big thing," I huffed!

Trying to calm me before I let the idiot sheriff have another idea of what I thought of him, Coop said, "Now darlin', it's not exactly helpin' the situation for you to be lightin' into the man the way you have."

Chastised, I replied, "He hasn't taken it out on you, has he?"

"Not in any particular way, but he won't share a cup of that coffee with me and breakfast wasn't any too good."

Rising and turning toward the office area where "the idiot" was making conversation with Jessie, I asked, "Sheriff, may I bring food in for my husband?"

"Well, ma'am, the town takes care of that sort of thing. It's all paid

"I see…. but if I wished to bring something in, may I?" I asked this in the sweetest manner I could tolerate at the time. I even attempted to bat my eyelashes a touch, even though it pained me to do so.

Jessie jumped on the bandwagon in like manner, "Oh, surely, sheriff, it would be all right to bring some meager sustenance to the poor man!"

"Well, I suppose it wouldn't be a problem, but I'll have to check any trays out before they go in the back."

Almost before he finished uttering those words, I left Jessie to keep my Coop occupied as I ran to the cafe and ordered up a large breakfast of eggs, bacon, hash browns and a couple sausages as well as a pot of their delicious coffee. All for my Coop! If he couldn't be free, at least I would make certain he'd be well fed!

The Journal of Jessie Llewellyn Harper

Poor Mary- and poor Coop! Mary was trying her best to keep from damaging the idiot in charge of the jail, finally succeeding in getting his permission to go and get some real food for her starving man (her voice was as sweet as treacle molasses and the creature succumbed!!). While she was gone, I asked the idiot if I could speak with his prisoner for just a few moments. He was reluctant, but I tried to look as woebegone as possible and pleaded with him for a moment with my cousin-in-law. He relented, so I went back to the cell and, thrusting my hands through the bars to catch Coop's, I said, "Dear man- Mary will be all right, I promise! I'm here for you both and always will be!"

He looked slightly relieved, but also a bit apprehensive, so I told him that my message to Vin had been as urgent as I could make it and I knew my Vin would be here as soon as he possibly could.

Coop looked at me and said, "I know he will, Jessie, I'm just worried that you and Mary might do somethin' foolish before he gets here!!"

"You can trust me, Coop," I reassured him. "We are both very level-headed women and quite capable of taking care of ourselves!"

He shook his head and muttered something that sounded like, "esporkytaynmeyado." Those boys have a devilish habit of lapsing into Spanish when they don't want us to know something! I must learn the language as soon as possible!!! When Mary returned, I went to the rooming house to try to think of something we could do if, for some reason, Vin were delayed or detained!

MARY

Jessie left as I returned to the jail. My Mama always said that 'honey catches more flies than vinegar', so I began shifting my approach to the idiot sheriff…

"Sheriff," I drawled, in my best Southern manner, "I thought you might like one of these fine muffins they had prepared at the cafe… just a little 'thank you' for letting me bring this over for my Coop."

"A muffin, you say? Hmm," he sniffed, appreciatively, "they do make some mighty fine muffins there."

Letting me carry the tray into the back, after checking it over, I took it to where Coop was ensconced in his cell. The aroma was divine to a 'starving man' and he was quite happy with the selection.

Leaning toward me he smiled and said, "Sweetheart, I see you've changed tactics!"

"If it gets me what I want, then I'll try it," I said with determination.

He just shook his head and chuckled. "I'm beginnin' to think I made a real good decision when I married you!"

"You're only realizing it now?"

At least I would be allowed to sustain my man food-wise. I made certain to always have a small tidbit and a smile for the idiot as well.

COOP

Now I had to stifle my laughter so as not to tip off the Sheriff… My gal had shifted tactics overnight and the adage 'Honey attracts flies faster than vinegar', or somethin' like that, has certainly been proven true. I realize I'm gonna hafta keep both of my eyes on Mary as she is real smart and downright tricky when she's after somethin' she wants!

At least it got me three square *and* tasty meals now. And don't forget coffee, the elixir of life!

The Journal of Jessie Llewellyn Harper

I almost ran back to the jail after stopping at the telegraph office on my way there! Vin had sent a response: "on my way" was all the wire said, but I felt a surge of relief and joy!! Perhaps he could be here by tomorrow morning! I couldn't wait to tell Mary and Coop that he was coming- not only would they be relieved, but happy for me as well! How I longed to feel his arms around me and hear his voice whispering, "Te amo, mi corazon!"

MARY

"Good morning, Sheriff," I said as I entered the office, delivering the idiot a fresh pastry. "Hope you enjoy." Choke on it is more like it!

"Well, thank you, ma'am. Let me open the door to the back for you."

"Thank you, sir," I nearly purred. Ick!

My Coop was standing at the bars waiting for me. "You look beautiful, darlin'."

"So now that I know how you feel about the breakfast, what about me?"

He laughed and said, "Come closer, sweet gal, and I'll show ya!"

I must admit I'll be happy when this mess gets cleared up and I can kiss my husband properly!

Taking my hand and kissing it, he said, "Vin'll be here soon. Don't worry..."

The Journal of Jessie Llewellyn Harper

After Mary returned from the jail (her new tactic of "the way to a man's heart is through his stomach" seems to be having a positive effect on the idiot!), we discussed what our next move should be.

"If Vin isn't able to convince him, perhaps we should wire the sheriff in that town in Colorado Territory," Mary said, a glimmer of hope in her eyes, "what was the name of it? I don't recall...."

"It's named after a tree..." I mused, "ah, now I have it – Willow... no... Willow Creek!"

"That's it!" she said, "If Vin can't convince that fool, then that should be our next move!"

"Maybe we can suggest that option to the idiot," I said, "if he does it, then he can't say we somehow tricked him by telegraphing a confederate or friend!"

"I'll plan to bring him a piece of pie with Coop's lunch!" Mary said, "I really hate placating him, but...whatever works."

I agreed wholeheartedly! Unfortunately, our request fell on deaf (or stupid) ears and we decided that we would have to do it, if Vin's persuasive abilities weren't sufficient to get Coop released!

COOP

My Mary, aside from makin' sure that I was well fed, sat on that hard ol' chair on the other side of the bars and read to me from a book she got from the library. As I lay on the cot, my eyes closed, tryin' to envision a time machine. I couldn't help smilin'... a time machine... some folks sure do have a wild imagination... glad she didn't choose some girly literature with all that flowery language... wonderin' how I got to be such a lucky man as to have found this woman!

Journal of Jessie Llewellyn Harper

I do not know whether to scream or cry!!! If I weren't so incredibly angry it might be funny, but it will take me some time to see the ridiculous in this situation!!! My dearest Vin, walking into the sheriff's office, drenched in the rainstorm this evening, carpetbag in one hand, slicker in the other- before I could even say hello, that cursed idiot had pulled his pistol and shouted, "Hands up, Cooper!!!"

I cannot believe that someone so irremediably stupid is still among the living!!! If Mr. Darwin is correct in his theories, this specimen should never have survived!!!! No matter how much we explained, and Vin's presentation of his Pinkerton identification (when the idiot finally let him reach into his pocket!!!!), idiocy prevailed, and my beloved is now locked into a cell next to Coop! That cretin of a sheriff, when presented with Vin's credentials, just growled, "That stuff can be forged!"

Now he has two "Jess Coopers" and seems to think that one of them will eventually confess and he will collect $5,000!! The thought of my Vin and Mary's Coop sleeping in a jail cell tonight, when they should be with us is making me too angry to even attempt to sleep! As soon as the telegraph office opens in the morning, I will wire the sheriff in Willow Creek regarding this crazy situation. I have also thought of telegraphing Sheriff Wilson in Laramie- he would surely know about Jess Cooper's past and, as they are good friends, would be concerned about this circular floating about! I have also thought of sending to the Pinkerton Agency in St. Joseph for verification of Vin's credentials! I hate feeling helpless! I vowed that I would not allow myself to ever feel that way again, and I intend to honor that vow in whatever way is necessary!

MARY

At one point during the night, I awoke to Jessie's pacing the floor, quietly muttering epithets aimed at a certain idiot sheriff!

"Honey, you need to try to get some sleep," I said.

Frustrated, she sat upon the side of the bed, releasing such a long, heartfelt sigh that I thought all air had been expelled from her body! She looked over at me. "I'm sorry if I woke you, honey."

"I've been going in and out all night myself...just waiting for morning when the sheriff opens up." I rose and looked out the window, dawn was arriving clear and crisp. Looking over my shoulder, I said to Jessie, "Looks like the cafe is open. Feel like coffee?"

"Why not," she said in resignation.

We waited, sipping a second cup of coffee and picking at a fresh out-of-the-oven muffin, opining what we could do now.

"We dare not telegraph Jess," Jessie said.

"Oh, no! That would be enough to send the oaf over the edge. Who knows what he might do with three Jess Coopers!"

"Probably think he could somehow arrange to collect $5,000 on each of them," Jessie jested.

"Unfortunately, I am worried just what he might do with our husbands once he realizes his mistakes..."

Concern written on her face, "Do you really believe he would do something to them to cover his mistake?"

I shook my head. "I don't know. He doesn't really seem the type, but he may feel pushed to cover it up..."

Considering possible outcomes, we watched for the sheriff to arrive at the jail. Paying the proprietress, we gathered the tray laden with food and fresh hot coffee for our husbands.

"Good morning, ladies!" the idiot sheriff addressed us jovially. Holding the door to the back room open for us, he seemed genuinely surprised when neither of us had an offering for him! He seemed about ready to remark upon the lack of muffins, when I turned and gave him my haughtiest down my nose look! It did amaze me slightly that he evidenced enough smarts to hush up and left us alone with Coop and Vin.

The Journal of Jessie Llewellyn Harper

I had not thought ever to have to kiss my love through the bars of a cell again!! As angry and worried as I was, at least we were able to share a kiss - not nearly as thorough as I would have liked, but "beggars can't be choosers!"

After I had explained, fairly coherently, in spite of my simmering emotions, just how this turn of events had occurred, I was thoroughly astonished when Vin burst out laughing!!

"I'm glad you think this is a joke, Mr. Vin Harper, but I most certainly do not!" I said, indignantly.

He reached through the bars and touched my cheek tenderly, although he was still chuckling, and said, "Mi corazon, we'll get it straightened out- it's just that nobody would believe this even if I swore on a stack o' Bibles!"

This set him off again, drat him- but once I tried to view it from his side, I did have to smile, just a bit!

He saw it, and said, "Little girl, I know how worried and upset you are, but just be patient - you'll get a telegraph from that town in Colorado and that'll clear it all up!"

"I devoutly hope so," I said, then whispered, "if that insufferable idiot can actually read!"

Vin laughed again, and said, "My little hellcat, you'll just have to teach him how real quick!"

"If that is what it takes, I'll do it!" I exclaimed, then I had a flash of memory and asked, "Vin, what does "essporkaytaygomeaydo" mean?" I think I reproduced what I heard Coop say fairly accurately, because Vin replied, " Es porque tengo miedo? It means 'that's what I'm afraid of,' more or less."

"Hmmph!" I said, "you must teach me Spanish, love!"

He looked at me questioningly and said, "Why? You plannin' on leavin' me for some caballero in Mexico?"

"I might consider it," I replied, "if I have to keep kissing you through bars, but that's not the reason. Let's just say I have an inquiring mind!"

"Little girl, I can think of lots better things to teach you than Spanish, " he grinned. "Just let me get outta here and I'll arrange some lessons!"

"I look forward to it, my darling, " I purred in his ear, "Just let's get you out of here first!"

I sent telegrams to Willow Creek, Colorado, Sheriff Wilson in Laramie, and to the Pinkerton office in St Joseph! If I could have sent one to the moon, I would have - desperation does things to my thinking processes! Anything or anyone who could get our boys out of this fix will receive a wire from me even if I have to sleep in the telegraph office!!

MARY

It was mid-morning and we could still hear the sheriff muttering about the smell of his favorite muffins on the air...Finally, just to get him quiet, I gave him two bits and suggested he go get a couple!

"Well, thank you, missus!" and off he went.

As I turned to rejoin Coop, Jessie and Vin, my eyes caught the glint of something half hidden under the morning paper. My heart beating rapidly, and looking around, I snatched the keys to the cells to my chest and darted into the back.

COOP

We all looked up as Mary entered, checkin' over her shoulder. She held up the keys to the cells, a wild look in her eyes! Jessie gasped and mirrored Mary's expression. Mind you all this occurred in a mere matter of seconds....

Mary ran to my cell, unlockin' the door and then passed the keys to Jessie. I'm sure the shocked expression on Vin's face mirrored my own! We both just stood there not movin' from our cells.

"Well what are you waiting for?" cried Mary.

"What do you think you're doin'?" Vin and I uttered in unison.

Jessie continued," How do you think the idiot sheriff will react when the telegrams arrive proving your innocence? I, for one, do not trust him!"

Vin and I looked at each other, shrugged our shoulders and exited the cells.

"Can y'all move any *slower*?" my wife asked in a peeved tone of voice. "Jessie, go get our stuff from the boarding house and I'll get the boys hidden and acquire some horses. I'll swing by and pick you up!"

With that, we made our escape.

VIN

I looked over at my cousin...Looked like he was as stunned as I was by the actions of our wives... Not knowin' what that sheriff might do if he came back while Jessie and Mary were in possession of his keys, I figgered it might be best just to go along with what was happenin'… and they made a good point about what he might do when the telegrams exoneratin' us came… of course, I had taken some precautions before I left Cheyenne...

The Journal of Jessie Llewellyn Harper

I peered out the door and looked up and down the street- no sign of the idiot! I walked sedately to our boarding house and hurriedly packed our train bags- not much larger than a pair of saddlebags, I thought, and slipped out the back door of the building. Waiting in the alley behind the house, I listened intently- no outcries or shooting, so I assumed that Mary had managed to hide the boys somewhere and had gone to the livery for horses. Sure enough, in just a few minutes, there she was with two horses!

We went down the alley and looked out surreptitiously in both directions- nothing but the usual afternoon lethargy of a small town was to be seen. "Where did you hide the boys?" I murmured.

"They're in back of the livery, under a pile of hay," she responded. "they weren't too happy about it, but I told them just to stay and be quiet until we got there."

"Good!" I said, "We can get there through the back alleys."

"That works," Mary said, "I'll give you a leg up."

We weren't exactly dressed for riding, but hiking up our skirts, we managed to get to the livery with no problem. I guessed that the idiot had decided to take advantage of his chance to sit in the cafe with coffee and muffins and ogle the pretty little waitress- kept him nicely out of the way, and had I not been so thoroughly angry with the creature, I would have wished him luck in his amorous endeavors! When we got to the back of the livery stable, Mary whistled (a talent I did not know she possessed, but with all those brothers I was not really surprised!) and our chaff-covered husbands emerged from their hay stack, looking as bewildered as two strong and able men could!

"Come on!" Mary said, in a kind suppressed shout, and they both looked at one another, shrugged, and climbed aboard the horses waiting for them.

We carefully rode to the edge of town and once we were out of sight, the gentlemen spurred their horses as if engaged in a race! Mary and I did the same, not quite as effectively, as our town shoes did not come equipped with spurs, but Mary's choice of horseflesh proved to be excellent -our animals had a fine burst of speed in them! By sundown, Vin and Coop assumed we were far enough away to deter being caught by any posse the sheriff might have been able to organize, so they set up camp.

Fortunately, although it was chilly, we had a small fire so the gentlemen could cook some rabbits (shot with our pistols, as Coop's and Vin's armaments were back in Adamsville with the idiot!). It was after we had satisfied our hunger and thirst (we had camped near a stream) that Vin looked at me sheepishly and said, as carefully as if he were "gentling" a tiger, "Little girl, you really didn't have to break us out of jail, ya know."

I sat up (I had been reclining against his shoulder, and was most comfortable there), and said, rather acidly, "You're welcome, I'm sure! Had I known you preferred a jail cot to me, I'd have quite cheerfully left you there!" I have no real excuse for my pettiness, other than the hard riding and the emotional turmoil of the past few days, but I had been so *very* comfortable!

"Whoa, now, mi corazon - I'm not complainin' - just wanted to fill you in on some stuff that I didn't get to tell you back there."

He then proceeded to tell me that he had left word with the Pinkerton agency that if he were not heard from in three days, they were to send an agent to Adamsville!

"Nice of you to tell us," I said, my tone even more acid than before.

"Why on earth, Vin, didn't you let us know?" Mary asked, from her seat close to Coop. She turned and looked daggers at her husband and said, her tone fierce, "Did you know about this, too?"

Coop had the grace to look sheepish also, and said, "Well, darlin' - Vin told me we shouldn't tell you in case you let it slip to that joker- and he was listenin' all the time you two girls were with us, so please don't take offense! We didn't want to push the guy into maybe a 'shot while attemptin' to escape' kinda plan for us!"

Mary and I looked at one another and, with dignity, arose from our respective seats and walked a bit away, out of the firelight.

"Well," I said softly, "Do we forgive them?"

There was just enough light for me to see Mary's grin as she said, "Maybe- in a little while!"

Shamefully, we both giggled and went for about a half hour's walk, being sure that was long enough to let the boys know that their behavior was less than satisfactory!

MARY

Having spent the night on the hard ground, but at least in the warmth of our husband's arms, I awoke a little stiffly to the sounds of birds singing all around us. The fire had been built up, as it was a very chilly morning. It was a beautiful place, this resting spot, and the stream burbled happily nearby. As uncomfortable as it was, I felt safe and happy snuggled in the crook of Coop's arms.

He must have felt me stir and he caressed my shoulder and back, "Mornin', darlin'. It's about time we get a move on... Jessie and Vin are up and at the stream gettin' some water for coffee."

I snuggled in deeper, "Don't want to!"

I felt, rather than heard, his laughter, bubbling up from his stomach, through his chest and finally his throat. "Have I told ya lately that I love you?"

"Hmm... Sounds like you're trying to get back into my good graces after that secret y'all kept from us, forcing us into a life of crime by breaking y'all out of jail!"

He laughed again, "Darlin', we just didn't know how to stop you two once y'all got rollin'!"

The Journal of Jessie Llewellyn Harper

It was a pleasant ride today, although chilly- Mary and I have "forgiven" our husbands for their unseemly reticence, and they have frequently expressed their gratitude for our enterprise and bravery in getting both of them out of jail unscathed (as they should!).

We have decided to sell the horses we "purchased" in Adamsville and take the train from North Platte to Cheyenne- Vin has sent a wire to the Agency giving them his whereabouts and requesting information from them regarding their dealings with the idiot. There is a comfortable hotel here, and after what seems like years instead of merely days, Mary and I would be able to sleep in a bed with our husbands!!

Imprisonment, jailbreak, running away from a theoretical posse, and camping out with little privacy would not have been my idea of a "wedding tour," but being with my dearest Vin was always much more important to me than the trappings of "civilized social necessities" (as Mama would no doubt say!).

After a filling and much relished dinner at a nearby cafe with Mary and Coop, Vin and I retired to our hotel room. "Now, love, " I said, "What about that Spanish lesson?"

He came up behind me and wrapped his arms around me (I could feel my indignation melting into other feelings entirely!) as he murmured in my ear, "You already know....te amo, mi corazon..." his lips were on the nape of my neck, and I began to have trouble remembering what I had been indignant about! "That's enough for now, little girl," he continued. "Let's spend our time studyin' something else tonight........."

MARY

"All aboard!" cried the Conductor.

The weather was much more seasonal, as it was a cold overcast day threatening snow as we departed North Platte. We had comfortable enough seats for the journey to Cheyenne and beautiful scenery to look at. We partook of a lunch of sandwiches and dainties from the cart which passed by.

"I don't know," said Coop, "if you ask me, it's highway robbery chargin' so much for these little ol' things!"

Of course, Vin was in complete agreement.

"Honey, I'm thinking it's time you teach me how to play poker," I quipped.

He looked at me a moment and then, remembering 'poker' was our 'code word', he said, "Yeah! Poker!" He reached inside his jacket and pulled out a ticket and handed it to Vin.

Curious, Vin asked, "What's this?"

I leaned forward and said, "It's y'all's wedding gift from us, the last Sleeper Compartment left on board!"

The Journal of Jessie Llewellyn Harper

Thanks to a very thoughtful wedding gift from Mary and Coop, our train trip to Cheyenne was most pleasant- I now know why she so highly recommended traveling in a compartment!! As much as I was looking forward to returning to Laramie, our train travel could have been extended indefinitely and I would not have complained in the least! Vin had received a wire in North Platte that reassured us regarding our status as "lawbreakers," with the promise of more details form the Pinkerton office in Cheyenne.

We decided to stay over there for a night, so Vin could collect his messages, and we would take the morning stage to the Raynes relay station where our horses had been cared for and stabled. The Pinkerton Agency had apparently routed the idiot- horse, foot, and artillery! According to their agent, not only did they convince him of our innocence and his stupid blunder, they also threatened to swear out a warrant for his arrest for false imprisonment! I must admit I am not a charitable person, as I spent a great deal of our evening in Cheyenne reveling in his comeuppance! I fear that I also had a satisfied smile on my face that had nothing whatsoever to do with the idiot and his well-deserved downfall!

VIN

I began to wonder about joinin' up with the Pinkerton's... there wouldn't be much time with Jessie afore I'd have to head back to Cheyenne... these past few days have sure been nice, havin' Jessie right there beside me...

MARY

Nowhere has ever looked as beautiful as did the Raynes Ranch and Relay Station as we rounded that big hill and pulled to a stop in the front! Jess was there to help the driver change the horses. Since we were going to collect our horses and ride home, we decided to pause for a bit and visit.

Coop and Vin watched Jess as he finished changing the team. When he was finished, they followed him into the house. Vin pulled out his badge and said to him, "I think we need to have a talk, cousin."

Jess' eyes got huge as saucers as he stepped back lookin' left and right like he might high-tail it out of there!

"Don't even think about it, boy," Vin said. "Seems we need to have a talk about a certain warrant for your arrest issued in Willow

Creek, Colorado."

Relief flooded Jess' features. "That was all made up and was over years ago!"

"Maybe so," added Coop, "but it sure got the two of us in a mess of trouble!"

"How so?"

We were all invited to sit around the table. Lilian Raynes insisted we stay for dinner followed by coffee and pumpkin pie as she and Bill both wanted to hear our tale.

"You busted them out of jail?" Jess exclaimed while laughing out loud at the thought. "I sure wish I coulda been there to see that!"

"Be glad you weren't," Coop said. "They woulda had to break you out, too."

"Sure am sorry that happened to y'all," said Jess, shaking his head.

Vin slapped him on his back, "Yeah, so are we!"

Jess stood and pulled a paper out of his pocket. "I been carryin' this with me ever since I was found innocent. It explains that wanted poster was all wrong and it wasn't me."

"That is all well and good for you, Jess," Jessie began, "but what are Coop and Vin to do? After all, the idiot ignored their identifications, even Vin's Pinkerton badge!"

"Guess I better ride in to talk to Sheriff Wilson and get it all worked out. Sure wouldn't want anything like that to happen again."

Lilian was so pleased for us when she heard the news of our marriages. Her husband, Jess, Vin, and Coop celebrated with rounds of whiskey at the boys' good fortune of finding such resourceful wives. Their son, Skip, was pleased to celebrate with another slice of pie!

It was beginning to get dark when we left these dear friends and headed home. Home, such a small word with such a rich, happy meaning. We would all soon be home! I couldn't help the fact that I wanted to show my husband off to my friends at the boarding house... even though most of them had been introduced to Coop before, it was now official!

Such stories Jessie and I had to tell. We had come out west to discover ourselves and independence, but we got a whole lot more than either of us ever dreamed!

VIN

I managed to get away from Cheyenne for a few days and go see my little girl... felt kinda funny, sittin' in Miss Emma's parlor again, like afore we got married. Miss Emma had asked one of her boarders to go up and tell my Jessie I was here...seems like a man oughta be able to go to his own wife's room, but Miss Emma is all proper, so I was just sittin' there, waitin', when she came into the parlor and sat across from me. She looked like one o' the school teachers I remembered – kind of reminded me of how Coop reacts to my Jessie when she gets her "schoolmarm" look, as I tried to sit up straighter!

"Well, Mr. Harper," Miss Emma said, "what do you have to say for yourself?"

"Ma'am?" I said, wonderin' just what she was expectin'.

"You come back, with Miss Llewellyn as your wife...quite a surprise for her friends! Did you ever hear the saying, 'Marry in haste, repent at leisure?' Seems like things happened rather suddenly, at least in your case," she said, stern faced and kinda disapprovin'.

I sat there, tryin' to think out how to explain it and she just stared at me…. I'd a been a lot more comfortable facin' a gunfight! I couldn't very well tell her that Jessie and me didn't wait for a preacher…. ain't the kind of thing a man says about his wife, that's for danged sure! After what seemed like a year, I finally said, just to say something, "I took a job, Ma'am, that was gonna take me away from her a lot, and I didn't want any man to think my Jessie belonged to anyone but me!"

"Hmmm," she said, frownin' at me, "so you think of your wife as property, young man?"

Now that made me hot under the collar, that anybody could think my little girl would stand for that, so I said, kinda short-like, "Not on your life! She's part of me, Miss Emma – and I'd give my life for her…. If I had to be away from her, at least she'd be married and safe… and I'd have her to come home to…"

I thought she was gonna get mad at me, but she just started to laugh!

"Young man," she said, smilin' at me, "I'm happy for you and your Jessie! Sounds to me like you'll treat her like the strong independent woman she is and value her for it."

"Yes, ma'am," I said, breathin' a sigh of relief. "We belong to each other, Miss Emma, like we was meant to be together. I'm thinkin' Jessie will be happy that you wish us both well."

"I do," she said, gettin' up as Jessie came in, "Here's your wife,

Mr. Harper - see you value her as you should!"

Jessie looked at me, kinda puzzled, and said, as we moved outside, "Vin, you look like you've been put through a wringer! What on earth have you and Miss Emma been talking about?"

"Just her congratulatin' us, little girl,' I said, "and makin' sure that I suited as a husband."

"Well, really!" Jessie said, frowning, "I should think that would be my concern, rather than hers…"

"She's kinda protective, I guess," I said, holdin' her close, "but so am I, so it ain't anything to worry about!"

She smiled and kissed me ….and I forgot all about Miss Emma…

The Journal of Jessie Llewellyn Harper

It is so good to be back in this beautiful Wyoming! I have missed the mountains, the cool evenings, and the wilderness close to my doorstep - being able to ride out with my Vin and enjoy the changing season is as close to Paradise as I care to come- at least at this time in my life! Mary and I are rejoicing in having our beloved husbands near at hand, even though my Vin will have to take assignments frequently for Pinkerton!! Thus far they have been "routine" (as Vin put it) and he has been able to come home to me after a few days. Coop has been riding "shotgun" (Western euphemism for "guard") on the stages between here and Cheyenne, so I have enlisted him to keep an eye on my Vin- he agreed, but said, "That works both ways, Jessie- Vin told me to keep an eye on you!"

"Why on earth?" I asked him, "I'm not doing anything dangerous!" "My guess is, " replied Coop, grinning, "he figures you might!"

Mary, who was sitting next to Coop in the parlor of the boarding house said, "Coop! Be nice!" and playfully jabbed him in the ribs with her elbow.

He pretended to be mortally injured and groaned, "Aw, darlin' - I was bein' nice! I didn't tell her the other things he said!"

At this, I pretended to be ready to throw a settee pillow at his head and all three of us started laughing uproariously! Vin will be home tomorrow, and I shall certainly find out just what was said- and he'd better not lapse into Spanish!!

COOP

"Tell me, darlin', when we get a place of our own, do ya wanna live in town or out on a spread?"

"Hmm," she began, thoughtfully. "I think I'd like to be near town but not right in it."

Pushin' her further, "How big a house you want?"

Takin' a deep breath and tuckin' her bottom lip in between her teeth, she smiled. "My perfect house would have a root cellar, a big kitchen and a parlor and at least three bedrooms," she said, a bit dreamily.

"Three bedrooms?"

Blushin' up a little, she said, "For the children."

"Well, why not four then? Or even six?"

"Looking forward to a big family?"

"Gonna hafta have a lot of hands to work the horse and cattle ranch me and Vin hope to have some day!"

Journal of Jessie Llewellyn Harper:

Mary and I had tea with Miss Emma the other day. Both of us owe her so much! She made us feel comfortable and safe in a bewilderingly new environment. yet there was something a bit sad about her… she has all her boarders for company, but both of us felt it.

"So, the two of you are married ladies!" she said, as she filled our cups. "I suppose you all are out house hunting…."

Mary and I looked at one another, wondering how she knew! She smiled and said, "I hear everything, girls. Keeps my life interesting, hearing all the gossip my young ladies bring home. By the way, some of them are about pea green with envy!"

"Of us?" I said, "Why? Just because we are married?"

"Partly," she said, chuckling, "but it's more who you are married to! Those girls are almost drooling over those two handsome boys you have under your spell! Reminds me of all the little cats who went into a tizzy when I married …. I wasn't the prettiest girl in town, but I managed to find the best man and marry him!"

"I didn't know you were married, Miss Emma!" Mary exclaimed. "We'd always just assumed you were a single lady, being called 'Miss' Emma!"

Miss Emma smiled, a little sadly, and said, "Oh, yes, girls. I had a wonderful man…he owned the hardware store back in my hometown – in Ohio, it was, and he was as good looking as those husbands of yours, 'cept he was blond, and he had the most beautiful hazel eyes…."

She paused, her own eyes misted over a bit and sighed.

"Tell us about him, please," I said, trying to imagine Miss Emma, the stern landlady, as a young girl in love, and failing completely.

"Yes, Miss Emma," Mary said, patting her hand, "do tell us!"

"It's long past," she said, patting her lips with her napkin, "but I can see him just as if he were right here in this room……"

Mary and I settled back in our chairs, teacups in hand as Miss Emma began her story.

"I was only seventeen and fresh out of the local school for young ladies," she said, her eyes seeming to look back over time. "Abel Hargreaves was twenty-five…inherited his daddy's hardware business at twenty-one and made a real success of it. I had no idea he was interested in me until one day when I was running an errand for my mama at his store… buying canning jars, as I recall…. I was asking him to put the purchase on the family account when he touched my hand and said, 'Miss Emma, there's a dance on Saturday…at the church hall…would you….um… would you like to go with me?" He was red in the face and having trouble getting the words out, but I was so surprised I just stared at him!"

She laughed at the memory and Mary and I smiled in sympathy. I thought about my embarrassment, pointing a hairbrush at my Vin... embarrassment seems to be an integral part of encounters like this!

"Once I'd made my tongue move enough, I said, looking down at his hand on mine, 'Yes…I …yes…I think…yes!' It's a wonder either of us ever learned to talk to each other, with a beginning like that!" She laughed, and we joined her. "We were married six months later," she said, "and, once we'd got over being shy, we'd talk about anything and everything together! When our children were born, Abel would tell them the most absurd stories to get them to sleep…."

Mary and I looked at one another - Miss Emma a mother! Maybe it shouldn't have surprised us, since she was much like a stern parent to the girls under her roof, after all. We didn't say anything, as Miss Emma had paused, looking back again into the past, her face saddened by some memory.

"We were very happy," she said, looking at both of us, "But fever took my Abel and our boys… it almost took me as well. I recovered, but I couldn't bear to stay there, in the house that had been so happy and was now so empty. I sold the hardware store to a friend of my Papa's and came West. Don't look so sad, girls," she said, smiling into our sorrowful faces. "I have a good life…lots of young company, this big house and plenty of folks in town I call friends. It makes me joyful to see my girls married and starting out to make happy lives…..just remember to love your men all the time….there's no guarantee you'll have them forever, so make the most of the time you've got!"

Mary and I both nodded, and chorused, "Yes, ma'am!"

"Now," Miss Emma said, "tell me all about your weddings! Why on earth you didn't wait 'til you got home to Laramie and let us all be there I'll never know – you'd best have a good excuse!"

COOP

We'd been in town several days. Miss Emma and the other ladies at the boardin' house were real pleased with the news that we were married. Now I figured it was time for the next step... Ridin' up to the boardin' house, I couldn't wait to see my Mary.

Takin' the porch steps two at a time, I strode into the house and found her in the parlor with Miss Emma. Takin' off my hat and noddin' to the ladies, I said, "Mary, get dressed for ridin', girl, I have somethin' to show ya."

She could tell how excited I was and just nodded and ran upstairs to change.

"Why don't you have a seat here, boy," said Miss Emma, as she patted the sofa cushion next to where she was seated.

Wonderin' what she had in mind, I nodded and took the seat she indicated.

"I have to tell you," she began, as she took my hand in hers, "how wonderful it is that you and Mary are married." Then pattin' my hand and smilin', she continued. "Being a smart young man, I am fairly certain that you have treated her like the lady she is."

She paused and leveled a look at me.

"Uh, yes ma'am?"

"Men!" she said, with what seemed like some exasperation. "I know it is none of my business, but the rapidity of your marriage is... disconcerting."

It took me a moment to see where she was goin' with this line of interrogation...

"Oh! No ma'am, it was nothin' like that! It's just that when I was at the fort and separated from her and then I finally saw her again, I knew that all I wanted was to have her as my wife and I didn't want to wait another second!"

She gave a little sigh. "Good boy."

I felt huge relief when I heard my Mary comin' back downstairs, dressed appropriately for ridin'. Noddin' to Miss Emma, I led Mary outside and we both climbed aboard my horse.

"Everything alright, dearest?"

"Yeah. I think so," I replied.

"Where are we going in such a hurry?" she wondered.

Smilin', I told her, "You'll see, darlin'," as we neared the Land Office. Dismountin', I reached her down and led her inside to introduce her to the agent there, Mr. Holbrook.

"Ah, Mr. Martin! You've returned!"

"Yes, sir, and I'd like to introduce my wife, Mary Martin."

"Madam," he replied, "a pleasure! Shall we take my buggy out to the property?"

Mary turned to me. "Property?"

"Just wait 'til you see it!"

Mr. Holbrook made polite conversation, but I sure wished he would go faster! The place was only four miles away but at the pace he set, it sure seemed a whole lot further! When we finally arrived, I watched Mary's face as we pulled to a stop. She took a moment to take in the view, then turned to me with that beautiful smile on her face that made her look like a young girl! I hopped down and helped her down, followin' Mr. Holbrook as he showed us the place. It had several acres with a little stream (at least at certain times of the year) and a yella two-story 4x4 house with green shutters.

Givin' us the tour of the place we saw that there was a good-sized kitchen, a parlor and two more rooms on the first floor. The second floor held four bedrooms.

"You were serious about looking to raise a large family," Mary giggled in a hushed tone and a glimmer in her eyes.

"You never know, darlin'. Best to be prepared though," I replied to her, grinnin' at the thought.

As we walked through the inside of the house, I couldn't figure out why no one had purchased it yet. … the price was sure worth it… sure there were some minor repairs and improvements to be made but I could handle those… even had a sturdy lookin' barn.

Goin' outside, Mr. Holbrook said, "This was part of a much larger parcel of land. It once included those two lots across the street, as well as a large unit to the east," the agent said while wavin' his hand in those general directions.

"That little buildin' there," I said, pointin' at a tiny shack across the yard, "would make a good place to store tools and such."

"Ah, well, ahem, that's the reason this place hasn't sold. You see, it is inhabited and the person living there confers with the property."

"*What*? A person '*confers*' with the property," I questioned, not sure I'd heard correctly. I wondered just how that could be legal!

"Yes, Mr. Ezra Buchannan. He used to be the foreman here- many years ago. The owners would rather *not* sell than evict Mr. Buchannan."

"Do you think we could meet him?" asked Mary.

A look of hope spread across the man's face. "Certainly. I shall approach him!"

After several minutes, Mr. Holbrook returned and ushered us to the 'cabin' to meet the gentleman.

"Ezra, these young folks are interested in buying the property."

Ezra Buchannan looked to be in his late sixties, salt and pepper hair and beard… he was wiry and his hands gnarled… with a slight stoop…

"They know the conditions put forth," he stated.

"Yes, I told you they were aware."

Eyein' us, he scratched his beard. "You got any younguns'?"

Mary spoke up in her gentle accent, "No, sir, not yet but we hope to someday."

"Hmmph," he turned and took a seat on a nearby stump fillin' his pipe, lit it and took a long drag. "It would be good to see lights on there and hear laughter again," he muttered, a cloud of sweet smellin' smoke billowin' around his bewhiskered old head.

Glancin' at my gal and gettin' a nod I said, "We'll take it!"

MARY

"Oh Jessie, you really have to see our new place! It needs some new curtains and a good dusting and airing out, but it will be so cute when I'm all done with it! The location is perfect for us, too- not exactly in town but far enough to feel like we are in the country! I know you've ridden past it plenty of times, but I just cannot wait for you to see it up close!"

"Why don't we go see it now," she asked, almost as excited as I.

On our way, I explained about Mr. Buchannan conferring with the property...

"Oh, my! I don't believe I have ever heard of such a thing! Is it legal?"

"He seems to be a lonely old man. The family we're buying the house from are just making certain he isn't thrown out into the elements. They must hold him in some esteem as they want to make certain that he keeps a roof over his head. He must be special to them...Once we move in, we'll have him over for dinner."

"I'm sure he'll like that!"

Upon arriving at our new house, I showed Jessie around.

"Can't you just see some gingham curtains hanging here at the kitchen window? And maybe some pretty blue ones in the parlor. I can see some cheery yellow ones upstairs ...Of course we'll need a variety of furniture..." A smile forming on my face, I said, "How about you help me go shopping?!"

"Now that sounds like a splendid idea!"

The Journal of Jessie Llewellyn Harper

I have put my share of Aunt Martha's estate to good use! The small ranch outside Laramie that we bought is perfect for Vin and me- I have even furnished it most economically (but tastefully!) with plenty of bookshelves and a comfortable settee and easy chairs in the parlor! Papa has apparently decided that he cannot have me committed to an insane asylum and has sent my books west, so I lack nothing for Vin's and my comfort! Mary and Coop are close by, and we visit back and forth almost daily! It may be tempting fate, but I hope and pray that my life here in the "wilderness" remains as delightful as it is at this moment! Vin will be home tomorrow - I know I will be wakeful tonight in anticipation of his arrival - any time apart is almost painful, but well compensated by the time we are together!

MARY

I woke early this morning in our new house, Coop sprawled next to me. The day was still dark and silent and peaceful… Sliding out from under Coop's arm, I rose as quietly as possible. Going downstairs, I stirred the fire in the stove and put on a pot of coffee. Walking to the window, I watched the most glorious sunrise, all shades of pinks and purples and reds. The adage, 'Red skies at morning, sailors take warning...' flitted through my mind and I was glad that none of us had plans on being any distance from home today, except, of course, for Vin. I sent out a prayer for Jessie's husband that he would be someplace safe and out of harms' way.

As the sun rose higher, it glinted like diamonds as it hit the ice-covered limbs of the trees. I sensed rather than heard my beloved approach. He placed his arms around me gently, joining me at the window, "It's a beautiful sight."

"It is," I replied.

Turning me towards him, "I mean you," he said, kissing me. It's amazing… this man can make me blush even after all we have shared, I thought, even as the coffee pot began to boil over.

COOP

The Ranch that Jessie purchased will be perfect for the horse and cattle ranch. Vin and I have been tossin' the idea around... Hearin' about some horses goin' up for sale in town today, I rode in to check 'em out. Would make a nice surprise for my cousin and Jessie...

"Well, Sheriff Wilson," I said by way of greetin', "expectin' trouble?"

"Let's hope not," he smiled. "Sometimes just makin' an appearance is enough to keep things quiet," he winked. "You thinkin' about buyin'?"

"Yeah," I replied, eyein' the stock. "My cousin and I were thinkin' of goin' in together on a nice horse ranch. Thought I'd surprise him with some in the corral when he gets home."

"I heard his missus bought the old Widow Smith's place. Good land out there."

"That's good to hear. I was worried she might've bought it on a whim. I should've known better though... she's pretty shrewd."

Findin' five nice lookin' horses, I bought 'em and herded 'em off to the Ranch. Jessie was surprised when I rode 'em in.

"Coop, they're beautiful, but what am I to do with them?"

"Vin will know, and when he isn't here, I'll take care of them! I couldn't leave 'em behind- they're too nice. They'll be perfect for breedin'. Besides, you'll be hirin' hands to help work the Ranch."

From the look on her face, I don't think she'd considered that far yet!

VIN:

Most o' my jobs for the agency have been nothin' much – spendin' a lot o' time on trains, overseein' bank shipments ain't exactly excitin', less some yahoos decide they want to get rich by stealin' 'em. Hardest part is bein' away from my little girl so danged much.

Last time I was back in Laramie, seein' the little ranch my Jessie found for us, made me even gladder I'd married her. It's right nice. Coop and me have plans for raisin' horses. It's got plenty of pasture land and a good barn with fencin' for two corrals, and I'm guessin' we'll need 'em… We'll need to hire some hands, once we get some breedin' stock – maybe, next time I'm home, I can do some lookin' around. Ain't that I don't trust my Jessie to hire good uns, but I wanta be danged sure I'm not leavin' her with a bunch of layabouts or no-goods… knowin' Coop and Mary are right close by helps some, but it ain't fair to put all of it on Coop.

I guess I was actin' kinda unfocused when I got to Smither's office today.

He barked, "Vin!" loud enough to wake a sleepin' bear!

"Sorry," I said, grinnin' at him, "Musta been off in deamland….."

"I know you're missin' that wife o' yours, Harper, but I need your attention on this," he said, not quite smilin'. "This job is gonna take all your focus, Vin – you'll be setting up as a shady character, and one slip could mean you'd not come back! The US Marshal's office there in Colorado has been trying to deal with the rustling ring for months and making no progress, that's why they've called in the Agency. I promised them two good men and you're one of 'em! I've got a man there already, but he needs the backup and I need one more man for undercover work besides you. I want three good men on this job…

you got any recommendations?"

"Ain't been with the Agency long enough to know many of the agents," I said, "no offense meant, but I don't trust somebody without knowin' more about 'em than I do now."

"How about somebody you do trust? Maybe we can hire him on," Smithers said.

"None close by, except my cousin, Coop Martin," I said, thinkin' about some of the fellas I'd worked with in the past.

"You think he'd be interested?" Smithers looked like a hound dog catchin' a fresh scent and I wished I'd not mentioned Coop.

"He's just got married, too, Smithers, and he's settin' up our horse raisin' business back in Laramie. Ain't likely he'd wanta run off for a month or two…."

"You can ask, Vin," Smithers said, almost beggin', seemed to me.

"Just what are you so all-fired anxious about?" I asked, "You got enough agents to choose from…"

"That's where you're wrong," Smither said, frownin'. "This office needs at least five more agents, what with the increase in settlement in this Territory, and I can't get 'em just by wishing for 'em! I need some real successes credited to the Cheyenne office – once they see we're on top of things and get results, the home office will authorize more hiring here. The Territory is growing, Vin, and there's a real need, but we have to show we can deliver the goods! This job, being called in by the marshal's office, is our chance to show we can do just that."

I thought about Mary – I know how hard it is for my Jessie to have her husband gone half the time and Mary'd be just as lonesome and worried as my little girl. But I could understand Smithers' point – the Territory was growin' and that drew in more and more no-goods, lookin' for easy money, just as it drew honest business men lookin' to carve out success. One day, Wyoming would want to be a state, but there'd be no chance iffen we were seen as too wild for civilized business.

"Tell you what," I said, lookin' Smithers straight in the eye, "I'll talk with Coop. But, if he ain't interested, it'll be up to you to find another man and I'll need to be certain sure I can trust him…"

"Fair enough," Smithers said, gettin' up and shakin' hands, "Wire me if he'll do it - I'll have him on the payroll soon's I hear from you."

He sounded almost too confident that my cousin would be doin' this, but I nodded and said goodbye. I just hope I ain't gettin' myself in trouble – ain't worried about trouble with the agency, but I sure as hell don't want trouble from Mary…or my Jessie, either!

MARY

"Somethin' sure smells good, darlin'." said Coop, reaching over my shoulder and snagging a morsel.

"Don't make me hit you with a spoon, Cooper Martin!" I replied in faux exasperation. "It's for Vin's homecoming and he and Jessie will be here soon!"

Shaking his head, "Well, I sure hope so 'cause I could eat a bear right about now!"

Looking my husband up and down I began to wonder, "You don't have tape worms, do you?"

Laughing, "Not last time I checked!"

Handing plates and utensils to him, I directed, "Put these around the table for me. It will make the time go faster!"

With a mock salute, he replied, "Yes, ma'am! As you wish!"

The Journal of Jessie Llewellyn Harper

Vin is home! It will probably be for a few days, as he has a job coming up that will entail his being gone for at least a month and some advance preparations must be made. I am not happy about that, but it is his work and he does not belong to me, nor I to him, in the sense of ownership - he is part of me and always will be, but we love one another for the darkness and the light - within and without ourselves.

When he told me about this assignment he added, "Little girl, how do you think Mary would feel if I asked for Coop's help with this job?"

"If I know Mary as well as I think I do, she will leave it up to Coop to decide," I said, "she trusts her man just as I trust mine!"

He smiled, and folded me in his arms, whispering "Mi corazon, I sure got lucky findin' you and I think Coop is just as lucky in his find, too!"

We are to go to dinner at Mary and Coop's home this evening - I am guessing that Vin will broach his request then. I do so hope that this assignment will not put him in too much danger, but I will not let him see that I fear for him - I cannot put him in jeopardy with worrying about me!

MARY

The four of us were enjoying some light conversation during dinner. "So, what are ya doin' to fill your time?" Vin asked Coop casually.

"Jess and Bill Raynes have rounded up a whole bunch of wild horses. They got a new contract for the Cavalry and I've been helpin' 'em break 'em."

"Just as long as horses are all you break!" I cautioned.

"Just about through with them, darlin'," Coop said, patting my hand. "Plus, there's the horses I brought out to the Ranch. By the way, cousin, what do ya think of 'em?"

"Haven't had a chance to look 'em over closely, but from what I did see they look dadgum handsome. But then, you've always had good taste in horseflesh." Vin cleared his throat, "I was wonderin' if you might be interested in pickin' up some good money helpin' me out with an assignment..."

Coop's ears perked up at that! "Tell me more, cousin."

COOP

Jessie and Vin had gone home, and I helped Mary finish cleanin' up. "Say somethin' darlin'," I said turnin' Mary towards me takin' the cloth from her hands.

"What do you want me to say?"

Liftin' her chin gently, forcin' her to look in my eyes, "What do you think of Vin's proposition?"

"I think it sounds dangerous!" She blurted out. Then collectin' herself, "Do you want to do this?"

"I do."

Closin' her eyes, she turned her head away. "You don't need my permission, Coop."

"No, but I'd like your understandin'..." I said as I caressed her chin.

"I'll not say 'no' if this is something you want to do," she said, placin' her hands on my chest.

"You know that I love ya, right darlin'?" I asked, as I scooped her up and carried her to our bedroom.

The Journal of Jessie Llewellyn Harper

It appears that Coop is willing to take on the role in Vin's assignment - I know Mary is a bit worried, as the "job" entails some danger - from what Vin explained at dinner this evening, there is large-scale cattle "rustling" (Western for 'theft!') occurring in the northwest area of the Colorado Territory which Pinkerton has been asked to investigate. Vin didn't go into very much detail - at least not at dinner! I assume that he will give Coop more information privately. I understand his reluctance to distress Mary and me or to take the chance of us accidentally letting slip information, but I wish I knew more! I suppose that my fears for his safety sometimes incline me to want to know more than I should about his work, but ignorance breeds fear - alas, I must curb my "enquiring mind" and accept that there are some things I will have to take on faith!

MARY

As I lay there listening to my Coop's steady breathing, I couldn't help but worry about this 'assignment'. It frightened me for some reason… I suppose it could be that we had finally found each other… and were newly married… making plans for a family and a future together… Perhaps it was just pure selfishness on my part… not wanting my beloved away from me for any length of time and possibly in harm's way…

The boys seem to believe that what Jessie and I don't know, won't hurt us… I would rather know what to expect than be left to guess… my imagination is very vivid and can lead my mind to all sorts of possibilities!

"What's on your mind, darlin'?" he drawled sleepily.

"Just the thought of you and Vin gallivanting who knows where and what y'all might be facing..."

"It'll be all right, sweetheart. You know Vin won't let anythin' happen to me."

Pulling me closer he kissed me. Bless the man, he sure knows how to communicate when the need arises!

The Journal of Jessie Llewellyn Harper

Vin has not shaved in three days! I'm not sure, yet, how I feel about his facial adornment - it does tickle a bit when he kisses me, but I believe I will get used to it for the time being.... although he hasn't said so directly, I believe it has something to do with this new assignment he will take on in a few more days. Coop remains clean-shaven, so I am wondering if Vin's new look is an attempt to dim their resemblance a bit.

Given Mary's response to Coop when he last grew a beard, I am most pleased that she doesn't have to endure one this time! Vin has also bought a new outfit - mostly black - it suits him admirably, I must admit, but I still feel a bit of trepidation! I have seen one or two men in Laramie whose attire is similar, and they appear quite dangerous - not just to me, either! The townsfolk seem to give such gentlemen a wide berth - just what is my darling going to be doing?!?

MARY

Coop and Vin rode out to the Raynes Ranch just after breakfast. I believe it has something to do with the "assignment" and while I am not thrilled about it, I know Coop feels compelled to participate. At least the boys will be in touch with each other during their time 'undercover,' as Vin put it.

I must ride out to the Ranch and speak with Jessie.

COOP

"So how long will y'all be gone for?" asked Jess.

"Don't rightly know," answered Vin, as he rubbed his chin. Seemed like that new beard he was growin' was itchin' a bit. "I appreciate y'all willin' to take on our horses until we get back. Until we hire on some good hands, I just can't leave them at the Ranch and expect Jessie to handle 'em."

Bill Raynes clapped Vin on the back and smiled over to where I was leanin' on the fence. "We sure understand, boys. We'd be happy to look after them for ya."

"Them, and the girls," added Jess.

"It does ease our minds," I said. "Mary ain't none too pleased about me taggin' along on this assignment!"

"Lilian will be sure to invite them over often. She enjoys their company. At least you know they love you," Bill said, sagely. "A woman don't worry about a man she don't love."

The Journal of Jessie Llewellyn Harper

"Little girl, "Vin said, as we were sitting down to supper, "I need you to listen close."

I looked at him, and almost saw a stranger! His new beard was trimmed to frame his mouth and chin and I was thinking how well it suited him, not paying much attention to what he was saying. "Hmmm?" I said, still admiring my husband, "What is it, love?"

"Will you quit starin' at me??" he said, laughing, "Feels like I'm under one o' those lens things that docs use!"

"I'm sorry, love, " I said apologetically, "it's just that I'm admiring your new look!"

He laughed, then quickly sobered, "Mi corazon, you need to listen real close, now, this is mighty important!" His tone was so serious that I began to worry a little! "This job that Coop and I are goin' on may take several weeks to finish, " he said, still very serious. "We're goin' to be investigatin' something that could get us killed if we aren't careful."

My hidden fears rose to the surface and almost choked me, so hard was it to keep from making a protest or urging him to decline the assignment!

"You need to know that we're goin' to be usin' other names and makin' out to be other men.... we won't be able to keep in touch with you girls except by letters and they'll need to be sent to a General Delivery - me and Coop will tell you what names to use and what town."

As hard as it was to keep my fear from showing, I believe I managed it..."I understand, love, " I said, as steadily as I could.

"If you don't hear from us regular, don't be scared or worry too much," he said, trying to be reassuring, but I could see that he was concerned.

"I promise, my love, that I will do my best not to, but I can't guarantee it!" I said, with a smile I tried to keep cheerful, instead of tremulous.

"I know you will, " he said, taking my hands in his, "just be sure you don't talk about this job to anybody! I'm on assignment with the Cheyenne office is all you need to know or say, if anybody asks, and you don't know exactly when I'll be back - that's true, anyhow!" he laughed and squeezed my hands. "I trust you, little girl, and you can trust me to do my best to keep a whole skin so's I can get back to you as soon as I can!"

I rose and came 'round the table - he reached for me and sat me on his lap - I put my head on his shoulder and said, "I will always trust you, my heart - besides, you still owe me that Spanish lesson, and an honorable man pays his debts!"

He laughed and held me close - no matter what our future holds, I am so very grateful to be loved by my Vin!!!

MARY

It's been two weeks since the boys have been gone. I have this terrible nagging in my heart, a feeling that something just isn't right… Jessie tries to keep me from worrying although I can tell she's just as worried for her Vin as I am for my Coop. Or should I say, Mr. Bobby Fullerton, as is his alias!

I have received the first of my letters yesterday. Not much is mentioned but it seems I am playing the part of his "best gal"! That fits…. at least I do have a General Delivery address, but I realize I must word my missives carefully in the event someone else should get their hands on them!

Mr. Bobby Fullerton,

General Delivery,

Winston,

Colorado Territory

Dearest Bobby,

I am so happy that you have found gainful employment at the K Bar K Ranch near Winston! The only thing that keeps me positive in your absence is the thought that the money you are saving up there will be for our wedding, so that means no card games!

My best friend, you know Jessie, she is missing her beau as well. At least we have each other to pour out our woes about our men being away.

I look forward to your next letter, dearest!

With all my love, Mary

COOP

Sat in on a game tonight which included my cousin. Managed to slip him a note regardin' the happenin's around the K-Bar-K... definitely somethin' funny goin' on there... lots of cattle showin' up that weren't there just the day before, then some brandin' on stock what looked like they had some markin's already...What irked me the most, though, was when I had the best hand in my life, and had to throw it in to let Vin take the pot! The things ya have to do when undercover!

There are a couple dozen men in the bunk house where I'm stayin'. Some look like mighty rough characters, not your typical cowhands... There had been one fella, kinda regular, but he disappeared one day. The foreman, a man named Tyrone, said he just decided to up and leave and what did it matter to me?

I told him. "Just that he owed me ten bucks from a card game the other night."

"Let that be a lesson to ya!" Then lookin' at me real close, he said, "You sure look familiar..."

I just shrugged my shoulders. "Ever been to New Orleans?"

Givin' me one last hard look he turned and walked away. Apparently, he couldn't place where he thought we'd met... good thing, but I remembered him... He had been along on a trip on one of the wagon train runs I'd done early on. Hopefully, I looked different enough now so that he wouldn't remember...

MARY

I have been attempting to take my mind off what my husband and his cousin might be getting into, working on some of the upstairs rooms in the house… Thank heaven for the company of Jessie, who came over to help sew some curtains.

"This floral pattern will look lovely in your bedroom," she said.

"You don't think Coop will think it's too girly?"

"I don't think either of our men care one way or the other as long as their girl is in the room!" she giggled.

It seemed she could always lift my mood when I needed it, as my thoughts had been drifting to the morose end of the spectrum.

Continuing on, "Are you using the same material throughout the upstairs or using a variety of colors?"

"I thought this one," I said, pointing to a pretty yellow, "for the room directly across from ours. The green, for the front one adjacent to that one, and this light blue for the one attached to ours. I'm hoping that one will be the nursery. Until that time, Coop can use it as an office."

She looked up at that. "Is there something I should know?"

"Oh, no… Just hopeful planning," I said with a smile. Then I just couldn't pretend any longer… "Oh, Jessie," I sobbed, my face in my hands, "I'm so worried about Coop!"

"Honey," she said, coming to sit beside me and placing an arm around my shoulders, "oh, I know… I wish I knew more about what's going on as well!"

"Yes, that's it! It's the not knowing!"

The Journal of Jessie Llewellyn Harper

I am becoming quite worried - it has been five days since my second letter from "Jay Vincent" in which he mentioned meeting a cowhand from the K-bar-K ranch named "Bobby!' I am in hopes of receiving a letter tomorrow - my dreams are disturbing me quite a bit, alternating between Vin and Aunt Martha with my ring or pendant in her hands! I am not generally a superstitious person, but this is the first time I have dreamed of her in many months! I don't think Mary has heard from her "Bobby" either - she seems low in spirits, but perhaps it is for the same cause as my less than cheerful demeanor - we both miss our husbands so very much!

MARY

I went to visit Jessie today as I am getting even more worried, since I have not heard from my Coop in several days! He had said he would be in touch every three days, and it has been a week since I've received his last message.

Sitting in her kitchen, as I sipped tea and, I'm afraid, mutilated a piece of pound cake she had placed before me, I spoke of my fears to her. "Am I being unnecessarily worried? Have you heard anything from Vin?"

When she answered that she hadn't any further information, I continued, "Jessie, I don't know why, but I just have a bad feeling! I'm hoping it's just because I don't know what's happening and nothing more serious!" Mashing the cake into little bits, "I *hate* feeling this way! Why aren't we hearing anything?"

COOP

Dadgum, but my head hurts… as does most of my body… wish Freeman would go away… and take Tyrone with him… Freeman just asks the questions… it's his foreman that has a mighty powerful right punch… They keep askin' who I've been in contact with, and how much Pinkerton knows… they can go to Hell before I give up Vin! Don't know what happened to tip them off… thought I was bein' so careful… sure hope Vin's safe… sure hope he figures I'm in trouble…

The Journal of Jessie Llewellyn Harper

"Dear Jessie -

Remember that cowpoke, Bobby, I told you about? Well, his girl lives in Laramie too - her name's Mary something (been up late winning, honey, so my memory is half asleep!) - maybe you know her? Anyways he was quite a player and I haven't seen him in quite a while - bad luck for me as he's a lousy poker player! Be a good girl, honey, and behave yourself!

Love, Jay"

When I read this, my heart jumped into my throat - "something's happened to Coop," I thought, "Vin wouldn't write this unless he wanted me to ask if Mary's heard from him or seen him!" I must go to her immediately! I hate having to worry her, but she needs to know!

MARY

There was a knock on the door. "Jessie! Come on in! I was just pouring a cup of coffee. Want a fresh out-of-the-oven cookie?" I asked.

I stopped dead in my tracks at the look on her face. "Jessie?" A feeling of panic began to wind its way up from my feet, keeping me rooted in that spot, my breath coming shorter, a sense of cold fear spreading through my body! "What is it?" I fairly screamed at her!

"What have you heard? What's happened? Is something wrong with Coop? Or Vin?"

She took me by the arm, propelling me over to the nearest chair. "It may be nothing, but Vin seems to be wondering if you've heard anything from Coop?"

Now I could feel myself begin to shake uncontrollably. "No! I haven't! Oh, Jessie! What could have happened?" I jumped up and began to pace now that I seemed to have regained the ability to perambulate…

Not being able to restrain my fears any longer, "Jessie, what if he's hurt or… or..." she held me as I burst into tears!

The Journal of Jessie Llewellyn Harper

My poor Mary!! She is so very worried, as am I! She burst into tears, my calm, controlled, Mary, and I had quite a time calming her down. Finally, after some "medicinal" coffee, we were able to talk about the possibilities of what may have happened to Coop.

Mary was determined to go to Winston herself - I thought about trying to talk her out of it, but I know her well enough that it would have been futile! So, I will go with her. We will travel under our maiden names and find some kind of lodging - there is probably a boarding house or such there - at least we will be closer to what is happening.

I am sure that Vin will not be pleased, but I believe I can convince him that we can be of help! Mary and I discussed our plans, and both of us decided that we would seek some sort of employment in Winston, indicating to the townsfolk that we were in need of such as we had lost our employment in Laramie - or wherever we decide to say we are from if anyone asks. It may be better if we say Cheyenne, or Medicine Bow, as Vin and Coop have been writing to girls in Laramie, and that might generate dangerous speculation. We can say we are half-sisters (as we do not really resemble one another!), hence our different surnames! If we find work, we will be in a position to hear things and can pass on information to Vin. That sounds like a very reasonable thing to say to convince him not to figure out a way to send us packing! Not only can we be of help, but I can promise to "keep an eye on" Mary (not that she needs it, but a small prevarication is sometimes necessary in perilous circumstances!) and prevent her from "doing something foolish" - I can almost hear my Vin saying that, and it brings a small chuckle! I am in sore need of something to lift my spirits!!

MARY

After speaking with Jessie and formulating our plan, I was ready to head out that very moment! Fortunately, Jessie's clearer head prevailed, and we made plans to leave tomorrow. It will be difficult to wait the extra time, but we will be able to get together supplies and plan more of our 'story'!

I'm trying to keep my mind on anything but what my Coop is going through, as my imagination is working non-stop on that topic! I'm afraid my dear friend will have her hands full with me! I'll ask her in advance for forgiveness for my future behavior!

Tomorrow we head for Winston in the Colorado Territory, and one step closer to Coop and Vin!

The Journal of Jessie Llewellyn Harper

Breaking our journey with an overnight stay in Fort Collins was a good choice - at least it gave us a change of scene and a sense of "doing something" instead of just sitting and worrying! I did a bit of shopping for our trip. Now that we have arrived in Winston and found lodging (a quiet and apparently clean boarding house run by a widow named Mrs. King), we have decided to begin our search for employment in the morning. I inquired of the Widow King (as she is apparently called by her boarders) if she knew of any employment available in town, as my sister and I were rather low on funds and wanted to be sure to meet our obligations. I could see that she appreciated our desire to be financially responsible and work for our living - I believe that Mary and I have demonstrated that we are honest girls and not riffraff! She said that two of the three saloons in town were usually hiring - I must have looked a bit surprised, for she said, "Dearie, I don't mean the type of work you seem to be thinkin' of!!! They do have girls to serve drinks and talk with the customers, but the proprietors don't allow immoral goings on in their saloons!"

I smiled with relief and Widow King said, " I'd be careful about the Lucky Diamond, though - that place sees some rough customers and ain't exactly peaceful on Saturday nights!"

Thanking her for her information and assistance, I returned to our room. I decided I'd keep the saloon suggestion to myself for a bit - Mary might not be comfortable with my plans!!

COOP

I've learned to be unresistin'… seems like they go easier that way… instead of startin' in on me today they were havin' a conversation… seemed odd, but I'm just so tired of everythin' that I just don't much care…

"This came in the mail today," said the foreman as he handed somethin' to the boss.

Freeman opened an envelope and read it out loud. It was from Mary! My Mary! How I wish I was with her right now instead of this cold rundown shack!

"Maybe this ain't the rat givin' information to the Pinkerton's," I heard him say. "And if it ain't him, who is it?"

"What do you want me to do with him?"

After a pause Freeman replied, "Keep him here for now. I need to think on this a while."

"I was hopin' for some fun," snarled Tyrone.

Shruggin', Freeman said over his shoulder, "Go ahead, just don't do nothin' permanent… for now."

MARY

The first thing we did this morning was to go around town trying to find employment. It was good fortune that I went to the local cafe for breakfast as they were in sore need of someone to wait on tables, as their waitress left town with her beau last night! While the proprietor/cook was also attempting to take orders, a back-up began to take place. I saw my opportunity and I took it! I stepped up to him and took his tablet and began taking orders. He wiped his sweating brow and murmured his thanks as he headed back to the kitchen area. Afterward, I helped him clean up and prepare for the luncheon crowd.

The owner, Mr. Timmons, was in his forties, sandy haired and bespectacled. He was so happy to have the help that he offered me a job! My hours would be from five in the morning to just after two in the afternoon as the cafe was only opened for breakfast and lunch. It's been a while since I had to be up and about at that time of day, but at least it should be a nice, safe job. A wide variety of folk patronized the place, so there was an opportunity of perhaps hearing something related to either my Coop or Jessie's Vin. Too bad I wouldn't be able to go with Jessie to help her find a job. It would have been more pleasant if we could have worked somewhere together, but at separate businesses, we would stand twice the chance of gaining more information!

The Journal of Jessie Llewellyn Harper

Now that Mary has found a job, I can put my plans into motion. Returning to the boarding house, I climbed the stairs to our room, treading as quietly as I could, as it was still quite early. As I unlocked the door, I caught a glimpse of a gentleman coming up the stairs, so I quickly slipped inside and closed the door. I don't wish to enter into conversation with anyone just now!

Unwrapping the parcels purchased in Cheyenne, I took out the dress I had chosen for my "interviews." A bright blue, trimmed with lace, and quite décolleté - I even found matching slippers and a fringed shawl that harmonized!! I had also found a coquettish hat (with feathers!!) to complete my ensemble! I don't possess cosmetics,

161

so I used a burnt match to darken my eyebrows a bit and place a discreet "beauty spot" on my left cheek! I had seen the girls in Laramie who worked at the saloons, and this outfit was comparable to theirs - not exactly provocative, but not "afternoon with the minister' garb! Now - we shall see!

VIN

I hated like poison havin' to scare Mary and Jessie by writin' 'em, but Coop's been on the job with Freeman long enough to have some information and I ain't seen or heard hide nor hair of him! Only reason I can think of for that, is that he's onto something and can't get away to meet me here in town. I've been keepin' my eyes and ears open in the saloons, but no word there either.... Might just have to see if I can get in touch with the other Pinkerton man out here. Don't want to spook anybody, but I'm getting' that crawly feelin' on the back of my neck again.... Thank God the girls are safe, back home in Laramie – worryin' about my cousin is hard enough - if those two were out here I'd be ready for the lunatic asylum! I love my little girl so danged much, and Mary is like my sister, but the two of them together scare the hell outta me!

The Journal of Jessie Llewellyn Harper

I have been successful! I now have a job at the Golden Horseshoe saloon. I am not sure that Mary will be sanguine about my choice of employment, but I was favorably impressed by Mr. Bart Ames, the proprietor, and his description of my duties. I am to serve drinks and "converse" with the customers - some of the "girls" live above the saloon, but they are not "working girls," and do not "entertain" the customers upstairs as part of the establishment's "services!"

Mr. Ames was quite comfortable with my remaining at Widow King's as several of his girls have done so in the past. I am to work Mondays through Saturdays with Sunday off. The pay is not large, but the girls are allowed to accept tips - fortunately, I am not really in need of funds, but this remains private between Mary and me. I report to work tomorrow afternoon. I must return to the Widow's and change into more casual clothing - it will not do to spill my coffee on this "working garb!"

COOP

Tyrone had brought friends in with him today, filthy bastard... he told me that they had my Mary... my heart sank at the thought... that they'd had their way with her... that she'd cried out for me... they almost broke me with that, but I knew she was safe back home in Laramie... safe... back home...

The guard... I've come to think of him as the 'nice' guard as he's the only one that brings food, if you can call it that, and water... came in after they'd had their fun... just tossed a plate and a mug in by the door... so thirsty... but just don't feel like movin' to go to it... too much effort...

Then there were hands on me again! I tried to shove them away...

"Stop it," he whispered, and a cup was brought to my lips. "Drink," he ordered.

The water was cool and tasted good on my parched throat. "Who... are you," I managed to croak.

"You don't need to know. It's safer that way… for both of us."

Then he was gone again.

The Journal of Jessie Llewellyn Harper

Oh, my! It has been a most chaotic afternoon! When I returned to the boarding house and began to ascend the stairs, I tripped on the hem of my "working" clothes and stumbled directly into my Vin coming down! His reaction was both delightful and terrifying!

"What in blue blazes are you doing here??!!" he exclaimed as he held me by the shoulders on the staircase, "Little girl, if I were inclined to do violence to a woman, this would be the time! You come with me, right now!"

He then pulled me up the stairs to the room across from Mary's and mine and dragged me inside! He wasn't hurting me in any way, just most insistent. I admit that I was both frightened and stimulated - I forget, sometimes, with his gentleness, there is also quite a bit of strength in that lean physique! At any rate, he plunked me down onto the bed and stood there, arms crossed over his chest, and positively glared at me!

I glared back and said, as coldly as I could, "I will be glad to explain, Vin, but I won't until you apologize for your behavior."

He looked a bit taken aback, but despite his anger, he began to grin, "Hellcat!" he said, eyebrow quirked, "I'm sorry! But you shouldn't be here, mi corazon! It's dangerous!" His grin faded as he said this, and worry replaced it.

"Believe me, love," I said, "I'm not here to be frivolous or interfere with your job - Mary was determined to come and I couldn't let her go alone!"

"Oh my God! She's here, too?? You two are more trouble than a herd of stampeding buffalo! Just what do you think you're doin'?"

He looked almost terrified, poor dear, but once I explained our motives and possible assistance, he did become a bit less upset, only remarking on my choice of attire with a rather stunned expression, "Que vestido!!" -- at least I finally got the warm embrace and kiss I was longing for!!

MARY

As I returned 'home' following the lunch crowd and cleanup, I discovered that Jessie had also found a job. "The Golden Horseshoe! Oh, Jessie, are you sure?"

"The Widow King and the proprietor both assure me it is a 'safe' establishment as far as unseemly activities go! It will be a gossip mill among the cowpoke who come in! I should be able to hear all sorts of things once they get a little inebriated!"

She seemed so truly thrilled with the position and the logic behind it that there was nothing reasonable I could think of to rebut her choice! "Just promise you'll be careful!"

"Oh, one other thing... I met the man who lives across the hallway… It's Vin," she said with a smile.

VIN

I swear, that little girl of mine is a handful! I dang near had a heart attack when I bumped into her on the stairs! I hate admittin' it, but she

can be a help in this mess... and who'd a thought she could look so
.... available??? Don't pay to underestimate a woman, for danged
sure!

Now I got her and Mary to worry about, as well as my cousin....
Come to think on it, though, druther have a woman with brains and
spunk than one of them empty-headed fashion plates, even if she does
drive me loco! Damn – I need a drink......

MARY

Poor Jessie, it was late when she got home last night, or was it
early this morning? I dressed quietly and made my way to the cafe to
get ready for the breakfast crowd. Mr. Timmons greeted me warmly, I
believe he wasn't certain I would return!

The cafe was quite a popular place, it seemed. A variety of
patrons passed through the doors in a matter of hours. There were
bank employees, the sheriff and his deputy, some ranchers, one of
the town attorneys, to mention just a few. There weren't many ladies
though until luncheon, if yesterday was the usual...

It was around nine o'clock when I noticed a familiar man come in
and seat himself at a table. I hadn't realized the hostility I felt towards
Vin for losing my Coop until just now! Striding over, I greeted him,
"What'll it be, Mister?" I'm afraid it was in a none too friendly
manner!

He looked up a bit surprised, but only briefly, covering up any
recognition.

Knowing his life could depend on my discretion, I continued, "Want some coffee while you think about it?" I still could not get that icy tone out of my voice!

"Uh, no, I'm ready. The special. And coffee. Thank you."

The Journal of Jessie Llewellyn Harper

I slipped across the hall last evening as I had arranged with my beloved in the afternoon -- Mary just grinned at me with a touch of sadness - she is so very worried about her Coop! After we had expressed our joy and contentment at being together by a protracted exercise of connubial bliss, I asked, "My heart, just where do you usually gamble?"

"I hang out at the Lucky Diamond, little girl - the boys there are just shady enough to be worth listenin' to."

"Oh," I said, "Widow King warned me about that place -she said it wasn't exactly safe, particularly on Saturday nights!"

"She was right, mi corazon - you just stay put at the Golden Horseshoe - I've got enough to worry about right now!" he said, rather severely.

I kissed him and promised that I'd stay at my own saloon and he could have his, but I needed to know so I wouldn't betray him to others.

"Sometimes, little girl, you're so danged smart you scare me!" he murmured, "but I get over it fast!"

I had intended to ask him about Coop, but he is very good at distracting me!!

Poor Vin! Not only is his wife working in a saloon and being ogled by cowboys, it isn't even "his" saloon where he can keep an eye on me! He told me that he had had breakfast at the cafe this morning and that Mary had waited on him - he wasn't very forthcoming about their encounter, but I could tell that she wasn't exactly overjoyed to see him! I know she blames him for "losing" Coop and I completely understand - perhaps this evening I will have my love come to our room (discreetly, or course), so he can give us some details about what has been happening! I am only scheduled to work until nine pm this evening as it is a weekday and even the most hardened patrons must arise early to go to their jobs!

VIN

I felt like I'd walked right into a blizzard! Even the cup of coffee Mary brought me couldn't warm up the tone of her voice and the look she gave me – I can't really blame her for it, though. I know just how she feels and I ain't got anybody but myself to blame for it. I wish she and Jessie weren't here, but I'm gonna have to use both of 'em to get this mess cleaned up and find my cousin…. Damn! Maybe all this "honest work" for Pinkerton is worse 'n sellin' my gun all over creation!

Feels like bein' caught 'twixt a rock and a hard place, like my Ma used to say…. but first things first. Mary has to know that I'll do whatever it takes to find her Coop, and much as I hate havin' her and Jessie involved, I know both of 'em well enough that they'd have it no other way. Sometimes I dunno if Coop and me got way lucky with our choice of women, or were just plain foolish! Lookin' back, life was much simpler afore I got married…. but every time I look into those eyes of hers, Jessie makes me feel like the world belongs to me…. maybe I shoulda stuck with the gals in the saloons, but a complicated life with my little girl is too damned good to lose!

The Journal of Jessie Llewellyn

Mary opened the door to Vin's knock and invited him in unsmilingly.

Vin looked at her and said, "Mary, honey, I promise you I *WILL* find him no matter what it takes!" He held out his hands and she took them, seeming to melt a little - he pulled her to him and hugged her, "He's almost as important to me as he is to you, Mary - do you think I'd deliberately lose him?"

The small break in his voice convinced her, I think, because she began to cry on his shoulder! Poor Vin - he just can't keep a dry shirt around us! Once Mary had calmed enough, Vin seated her in the chair and came to sit beside me on my bed. "I know you both came here because you felt you had to," he began, "and I was real upset when I found out, but I do think you can be of help to me and Coop."

I smiled a bit complacently – fortunately, Vin was looking at Mary and not me, so I had time to compose my features into a more appropriate expression of interest!

"We had decided," Vin continued, "that Coop would pose as a driftin' cowhand lookin' for work - he'd need to appear a bit shady, 'cause he was goin' to ask for a job at Jake Freeman's K-bar-K ranch. We suspect Freeman of bein' in on this rustlin' - he's got way more money and sells more cattle than he should, based on the size of his spread. Coop went out there and got hired on - he'd come in to the Lucky Diamond to play poker, bein' careful to lose and get riled about it when he was playin' with me."

Mary and I were listening intently, as Vin continued. "Well, about two weeks ago, he stopped comin' into town. Nobody said anything about him, but there were a couple of K-bar-K hands that kinda grinned at each other when I mentioned his name. They didn't really say anythin', just kinda smirked, so I got some worried. I thought maybe he'd gone back to Laramie 'cause he'd heard from you, Mary, and you needed him for some reason. I didn't think he'd go without tellin' me, but if it was some kinda emergency...... so that's why I wrote Jessie the way I did. I figured she'd catch on and let me know if he was there."

He looked sideways at me with a severe expression, " I sure didn't expect you two to show up here in Winston, hot after my hide!"

Mary blushed a little remorsefully and said, "I'm sorry, Vin - I've just been so very worried about him!"

"That's OK, honey, " he said, smiling at her, "I do understand! Just want you to know I'm worried, too!"

"What do you think has happened to him, Vin?" I asked, almost afraid to hear his answer. "I think he's in big trouble, but alive," Vin said, considering. "He's made some friends among the hands - the more honest ones -and none of 'em have asked after him, so that could mean he's still out at the ranch and, for some reason, can't get to town."

"How can we help, Vin?" asked Mary, hands clasped tightly in front of her.

"You girls can listen, " he said, looking from one to the other of us. "Folks talk in saloons and in the cafe - keep your eyes and ears open and come tell me on the quiet anything you see or hear!"

"We can do that, love, " I said, "are there any particular people we should be looking or listening for?"

"Jake Freeman!" Vin said, promptly, "he doesn't often come into the Diamond, but he's a regular at the Golden Horseshoe! He eats at the cafe at least a couple of times a week, too." He looked at me, almost admiringly, "I dunno how you do it, mi corazon - you're either the luckiest woman I ever met or the smartest - both of 'em scare me a good bit!"

I laughed and kissed him, "I'll remember that, my heart, next time you get mad at me!"

We decided that we'd arrange another "meeting" after Mary and I had a couple more days at our jobs - giving us a chance to learn about some of the people of Winston and watch for Mr. Freeman!

COOP

It must be night... it gets even colder in here at night... and they stop usin' me as a punchin' bag... seems they might have somebody else they're interogatin' instead of me since nobody's been in today. Or maybe they're just toyin' with me... thinkin' I'll feel safe and reveal somethin'... Sure as Hell wish I hadn't told Vin I'd help with this assignment... should be layin' in my Mary's arms... all safe and secure and… not hurtin'… not freezin' in this stinkin' shack... got a real bad feelin' about how this has turned… my only hope is that Vin busts through that door and takes me back home… just hope I'm still alive when he gets here…

MARY

Working at the café, I noticed when a man, accompanied by three other men who looked like personal guards, came in for breakfast. I asked Mr. Timmons who he was, and he replied that he was Ed Freeman, a 'big spender'! Formulating a quick plan and keeping my fingers crossed that it would work, I approached his table.

"Excuse me, are you Mr. Freeman of the K Bar K Ranch?"

Surprised, he looked up at me and gave me a puzzled smile. "Yeah, honey, I am. Is there somethin' I can do for you?"

Pretending to be shy and unsure, "Oh, sir, I certainly hope so! You see, my fiancé sent word that he had gotten a job at the K Bar K about a month ago. He was writing real regular and then suddenly the letters stopped coming! Do you know anything about him? His name is Bobby Fullerton, and we're to be married once we can save up enough money...Oh, please, do you know him?" I blurted this out in my best 'girl in distress' mode.

There were glances all around the table. One of the men almost spit his coffee but managed to swallow instead, covering his reaction by muttering something about it being too hot!

"You say he's your fiancé?"

"Yes, sir."

"I do recall a man by that name. I believe he is on a cattle drive for the ranch right now..."

"Oh, goodness! That's such a relief! So, he's all right?"

Freeman smiled, "Yeah, honey, he's all right."

I took their orders and tried to listen in their conversation when I could. I think I heard 'Bobby's' name mentioned. When they had finished the meal and were ready to pay, I told Mr. Freeman that his meal was on me as he relieved my mind so much!

This seemed to make him happy and he responded, "I'll make sure that fiancé of yours sends word!"

Throwing my arms around his neck I gave him a peck on his bearded cheek, "Oh, thank you!"

The Journal of Jessie Llewellyn Harper

We must do something!

As I passed Jake Freeman's table in the Golden Horseshoe tonight, carrying drinks to the one immediately adjacent, I heard him say "Fullerton!" I slowly distributed the beverages on my tray, smiling as much as I could at each gentleman and moving as slowly as I dared.

"He was writin' to his girl?" said one of Freeman's men (a large, uncouth -looking fellow), "maybe he ain't the one we're lookin' for!"

Another responded, "Tyrone said he knew him from somewheres and didn't believe he was just a drifter."

"Tyrone ain't exactly real truthful all the time," said another (smaller, but with a sly expression and beady dark eyes).

As I was about to place the last of my tray's contents on the table, I heard Mr. Freeman say, "If he's not a spy, then he knows too damned much! Get rid of him - permanently!"

My heart nearly stopped!

"OK, boss," said the large one, "he still at the line shack by Sommer's Creek?"

"Yes - and don't waste time! We've got way too much riding on next week's job to take any chances!" said Freeman, with a glare at his henchman.

I was almost in a panic… I remember thinking, "I've got to tell Vin... and Mary," and trying to think of a way I could escape and do so when a lucky stumble on the part of a rather inebriated gentleman (the bank teller, I think) caused me to stumble and fall! Thank fortune, I was not hurt, but my chance to escape was mercifully provided!

I stood up, shakily, wincing with pain, and said to my boss, "Oh, sir, I seem to have twisted my ankle! I am so sorry to be so clumsy!"

Mr. Ames said, most kindly, "You go on home, Miss Jessie, and take care o' that ankle - there're enough girls to cover the place tonight."

I thanked him and limped as painfully as I could to the doors, exited, and lifted my skirts and ran!

When I reached the boarding house, Mary was in our room. I blurted out what I had heard and, as expected, she said, "Quick - get out of that dress and into something you can ride in, just in case!"

I did so, still shaking a bit, and we went to the Diamond to see if Vin was there - he wasn't, and we had no idea where he could have gone! We'd checked his room before we left the boarding house, so our only recourse was to try to find Coop on our own!

Mary has gone to the livery stable - thank fortune my mishap and news collection had happened early in the evening, as the hostler usually stayed until about nine to see to the horses of those who were still "entertaining" themselves in town. I have written a note to Vin and secreted it under his pillow (he gave me a spare key!) where he will surely find it when he comes in. Now we just have to find the "line shack" where they have Mary's Coop!! We are both armed – God grant we get there in time!!

VIN

I'd made arrangements through Smithers for gettin' a meetin' with the Pinkerton man they'd sent out first… mostly outta hope that he'd not been taken out afore Coop and me got here. There was what they call a "drop off point" just outside o' town where a note could be left for pickup in case of an emergency. When I got there, there was a fella camped pretty near. I was in tow minds about bracin' him – coulda been just a drifter or a ranch hand, but I was gettin' right worried about my cousin, so I figured I'd best chance it. I called out, "Hello the camp!" Kept my hand on my gun just in case….

"Howdy!" came back, "Light and set if you've a mind to."

"Got any coffee?" I asked, as I dismounted and ground-tied my horse.

"Sure!" the fella said, grinnin' at me, "Got plenty – and cold biscuits…..you ever et peach jam on a cold biscuit?"

I don't think anybody coulda heard my sigh of relief…felt loud to me, but I don't guess it carried too far, cause the fella was still grinnin'. "Cold biscuits and peach jam"- meant this was our Pinkerton agent!

"I'm Harper, from the Cheyenne office… glad you showed up, mister!" I said, sittin' down on one o' the logs he'd drawn up beside his fire.

"I'm Randall," he said, "glad to meet ya, Harper. I got some bad news for ya…"

"Oh, Lord," I thought, wonderin' how I was to go back and tell Mary her man was dead! "Spit it out, Randall, I'm listenin'."

"Freeman's got real bad suspicions about a hand named Bobby Fullerton," he said, "thinks he's an informer or maybe a lawman and he's given his men orders to kill the guy as soon as they sweat the truth outta him. I know he isn't from the Agency, and there's no other law enforcement fellas out here – US Marshal's office agreed to stay out and leave this to the Agency. They got him hid in a line shack on Sommer's Creek."

"He's one of ours," I said, "my cousin, as a matter of fact and doin' this job mostly as a favor to me! Can you get back to him and do your best to keep him alive until I can get there?"

"Yeah, sure can," he said, "You got anybody else out here 'sides him workin' with you?"

"In a kinda way," I said, not wantin' to tell him about Mary and Jessie gettin' themselves involved in a Pinkerton case, "Why?"

"Just don't want to have anybody besides you to know about me 'til we get this wrapped up, Harper," Randall said, right serious-like. "If Freeman is havin' suspicions enough to kill a man just on one of his boys thinkin' he knew him from somewhere, I'm not real interested in bein' known by anybody as a Pinkerton!"

"You got my word, Randall – nobody'll know from me, 'less you tell me different!" I said, "Now I need you to get out there and keep my cousin alive 'til I get there – OK?"

"You got it!" he said and started to gather up his stuff and pack it on his horse.

"Don't take too long, Harper," he said as he mounted and headed off, "I'd like all of us to get this case taken care of and still be alive when we do!"

I nodded and headed back to town…. I knew I'd need a fresh horse and my rifle….

MARY

We rode as quickly as we could and still be considerate for our safety and that of our steeds. Fortunately, it was nearly a full moon out tonigh,t even though it was almost bitterly cold, and clouds were forming!

About a mile from the 'line shack,' we found a small area offering concealment for the horses. As we approached Sommer's Creek, it became apparent that it was more of a small complex than only a line shack! But there was one small building which was guarded. Jessie and I both exchanged silent communication that this was where we would begin our search! Sneaking around and down by the back of this building, we heard someone come by and ask the guard if all was well with the prisoner and something about not needin' to worry about him much longer!

Waiting for this other man to walk away out of sight, we approached the guard from the rear and Jessie placed her revolver in his ribs. "Nice and slow now. We're all going go into this shack," she said as I removed the man's weapon. We slid silently through the door and I almost let out a scream! My poor, darling Coop! I ran to his side, his head was lolling on his chest, his face battered and bloodied! The poor dear moaned and tried to bat away my hands...

The simpleton guard laughed at the reaction! Knowing we would have to do something with this man, and a bullet would make too much noise, bringing his compatriots, I told Jessie I'd be a moment as I stepped outside, and returned with the cast iron frying pan from which I had noticed the guard had been eating. I swung it for all I was worth, just trying to get some pay back for my beloved! I was rewarded with a good solid 'thunk' as it connected neatly with the back of the miscreant's head and he fell like a sack of potatoes to the ground.

With a look of awe, Jessie asked, "Do you think you killed him?"

Shaking my head, "I don't know and quite frankly, I don't care!"

While I began checking my Coop, Jessie took the place of the guard out front by the door, so no one would get suspicious if they noticed he was missing.

Coop started to stir and let out a small moan before he could control it.

"It's alright, beloved, we're going to get you out of this."

His head turned in my direction, and he looked at me with surprise and then panic! "What...how...who...no! You need to leave! You can't be... here... You can't be... caught here..."

"We are going nowhere without you! They are going to kill you!"

He laid his head back and digested this information, looking at me through his right eye, as his left was so swollen from the bruising!

"Can you walk if I help you?"

"Yeah, I think so… Guess I'll... have to…"

Aiding him to a standing position was more difficult than either of us thought, but we managed.

Tapping gently on the inside of the door, Jessie opened it from the outside for us. She gave us the 'all clear' and grabbed Coop from his other side. He bit off a moan as we hobbled our way back to our horses.

Coop was close to a state of unconsciousness, only staying upright through sheer determination! It took both Jessie and me to get him onto my horse and me up behind him. As we started for town the snow began to fall...

COOP

The hands were at me again! No….

"It's alright, dearest, we're going to get you out of this."

Mary? I must be delirious!

"What...how...who...no! You need to leave! You can't be... here! You can't be… caught here..."

Panic filled my heart and soul! I must get her to leave! If they find her, they'll… they'll…

"We are going nowhere without you! They are going to kill you!"

Kill me? Yeah, I can understand that... Figured that was a possibility...We?... I'll tar and feather Vin if he brought her into this... so difficult to just stand up... even with Mary helpin' me... so tired... God, I hurt... Jessie...What?... If I can just make it onto that danged horse…

The Journal of Jessie Llewellyn Harper

Coop was barely able to stay in the saddle, even with Mary holding onto him, so, once we were several miles away from the line shack, I pulled up in a small grove of trees and we helped Coop to dismount. Mary had brought some elementary medical supplies, just in case, and we were working by moonlight (we didn't dare have a fire!) to clean up some of the poor man's cuts and bruises, when I heard a horse coming. Putting my finger to my lips, I looked at Mary, who promptly put her hand over Coop's mouth - he was unconscious, but she didn't want an unexpected groan or moan to give away our presence. We remained crouched in our positions under one of the trees, as the rider slowly approached us.

One of the horses nickered, and Mary and I prepared to use our pistols. Most fortunately, before we fired, I recognized my Vin! He came to us, looking, from what I could see in the moonlight, both relieved and angry enough to bite someone!

"Beloved, "I whispered, almost too surprised to form the words, "we had to - we couldn't find you and they were going to kill him!" I couldn't keep my voice from shaking and just looked at him, tears rolling down my face!! So much for being cool, collected, and heroic!!

God bless my dearest Vin - he just picked me up off the ground, held me close, and whispered in my ear, "Thank God you're all safe! Mi corazon, what am I gonna do with you?!?" and then he kissed me as if he'd never stop!

I suppose being less than cool, calm, and heroic has its compensations - it certainly did tonight! Once he had finished kissing me (I forgot about poor Coop and Mary for those few moments - Vin's kisses have that effect on me!), he knelt down to look at Coop. "He'll make it, honey," he said to Mary," I heard somethin' in the Diamond tonight that brought me out here - some fella named Tyrone was braggin' about a 'spy' to some o' the K-bar-K crowd, and I knew they had a place out here from other stuff they said, so I figured I'd take a looksee. I'm sorry, Mary, that you couldn't find me - I was trying to do what you two have already accomplished!" He looked at both of us and said, with exasperation and just a hint of admiration, "I swear, you two are almost too much for an ordinary man to handle!"

"Isn't it lucky, love, that you and Coop are such extraordinary men?" I said, leaning into his shoulder as he got up.

"I'm guessin' we must be!" he laughed, "Let's get Coop back to town so the doc can have a look at him!"

"The sooner the better," scolded Mary, "you two can compliment each other all you want as soon as I get this one taken care of!"

We got Coop up on Vin's horse - much easier with Vin to help! - and Vin rode behind him on the way back to town, Coop came to for a bit and I heard him say to Vin, "Cousin, we gotta do somethin' about these women o' ours..."

Vin just said, "Coop, I hate to tell ya while you're hurtin', but I don't think there's a doggoned thing we can do except love 'em and keep a close eye on 'em!"

VIN

When I'd got to the camp on Sommer's Creek, it was hummin' like a knocked over beehive! I'd come up on it as quiet and roundabout as I could - tied my horse in a stand of trees close by where I figured they had Coop. I was crouched down behind a clump of bushes and watchin' Freeman's boys millin' around, when I felt a hand on my shoulder –

"Harper! It's me, Randall… stay still!" came a harsh whisper and I eased my gun back into the holster.

"You nearly got yourself shot!" I whispered back, hissin' like a stepped-on snake.

I heard a soft chuckle and then Randall said, "Glad you slowed up a bit, Harper – your man ain't there! Somehow, he managed to get away – dunno how, though…he was mighty beat up. Seems he took the guard down with a fryin' pan or somethin' – that's one tough cousin you got, Harper!"

"You could say so," I said, "Any idea which way he went?"

"Nope," Randall said, "but it had to be around back of that line shack down there, otherwise I'd a seen him – the guard was still outside when I came by to check. I can't go with ya, gotta keep my cover, but try trackin' him from there…"

"Thanks, man" I said and slipped back into the trees as Randall gave a wave and sidled around the brush, callin' out, "No sign up here, boys…"

Damn! I thought, maybe Coop's not as bad off as Randall thinks.

MARY

Vin had the idea that we shouldn't return to Winston. "I think you three had better disappear for now, it'll be safer for all concerned."

He traveled with us to a small town named Brackettsville about nineteen miles north of Winston with the snow beginning to fall heavily. Settling us into the only hotel there, he brought the doctor to us and headed out. He wanted to get back to Winston before sunrise.

Jessie saw her Vin on his way as the doctor was finishing up with my Coop. He rose and patted my hand, "He's going to be hurting for a while. I set the broken nose and wrapped his chest just to splint the ribs some. Once most of the swelling reduces, he should feel much better. He needs rest and care. He's running a fever, most likely as a result of the trauma. Try to keep him as hydrated as he'll let you. When he can, let him eat whatever his mouth lets him have. He'll be tender for a while so only soft foods to begin with."

As I was thanking him, he departed, and Jessie came back in asking solicitously, "How's he doing?"

I filled her in, and we decided we'd all settle in for a much needed rest.

There were two beds in the room. Jessie took one and Coop and I, the other. It was a couple hours later when I awakened to Coop thrashing about feebly. "Hush, dearest, hush," I said as I stroked his forehead. "You're safe, you're safe..." He seemed to understand even though he was still unconscious. He sighed, nestling into my embrace.

COOP

Mary... Mary's here... can't let her be caught!... Must be a dream... yeah... finally a *nice* dream. I can almost feel her and hear her sweet liltin' voice... hurts to try and breathe deep... hurts to think... so don't! Chase that dream, boy... might be the last good thing you have before they kill ya... Mary... wish I *was* with my Mary... in our own bed... so soft... finally found a good woman to love me and it all ends like this... damn...

The Journal of Jessie Llewellyn Harper

It was so hard to see Vin off - I had hoped he'd stay the night, or at least the rest of it, with us, but he was anxious to return to Winston and get in touch with the US Marshal who had requested the Pinkerton Agency's help. He also wanted to be sure that no one knew of our part in Coop's escap,e and promised he'd speak to Mrs. King and pay our board.

"She's an honest lady, " he said to me, just before we said goodbye, "I'll tell her that you two were called away - family emergency - and have her send your things on to Laramie. You stay here with Mary and Coop and I'll telegraph as soon as I can. Promise me, little girl," he said, looking a bit anxious, "you won't go harin' off somewhere without tellin' me!"

"Of course, I won't, love!" I said, indignantly, "We wouldn't have done what we did if it hadn't literally been a matter of life and death - and, we *did* try to find you first!!"

He put his arms around me and held my head against his shoulder, saying in a voice that was not quite steady, "I know, mi corazon, and I'm real proud of you and Mary, but you scare me so! I couldn't bear losin' you, little girl...."

"You won't, my heart, if I can do anything about it!!" I said, brushing that vagrant curl off his forehead. "You are my light, love, and I promise I will always try to keep from darkening it by my actions! You must know, though, that I gave up being a "timid little rabbit" shortly after we met, and I'm very sure I can't go back to being one!"

"Just so's you tell me, honey, before you go chasin' dragons!" he murmured, holding me close.

"I promise, love - after all, that is supposed to be your job!" He laughed and said as he went out the door, "So long as you remember that, little girl, we'll both sleep easier!"

I waved, and he was gone. I went back to our room to see if Mary needed any help with Coop - thank God, at least they would spend tonight together.

MARY

"No!" Coop shouted in the predawn.

I tried to calm him, but he shoved me away!

Falling out of the bed, I felt my temple hit the bedside table.

"Jessie! Get the lamp lit!" I implored, as I picked myself up off the floor. "It's alright dearest," I crooned to him as I neared.

He thrashed about, trapped in some private Hell, battling those demons spawned by the pain fever and his recent experiences. He then began to tremble all over, calling out my name. I grabbed the compress to place back on his forehead. "It's alright, dearest. You're safe now. It's alright..."

His brief bout of energy now spent, he quieted back down. I caressed his face, gently reinforcing that he was safe, it was all over.... and so, the rest of the night went.

As the morning broke, so did Coop's fever and the torments which went with it! He opened his eyes and seeing me gave me a weak smile. "I thought... I heard... your voice," he murmured. "You were... way away... in... the distance... I latched on to it..." and he fell back asleep holding my hand.

The Journal of Jessie Llewellyn Harper

Mary has a bruised cheek this morning - poor Coop has been fevered all night and, in delirium, pushed her out of bed and onto the floor! Thank fortune, his fever broke this morning, and I believe he will soon regain his strength. Those fiends beat him very badly and I have a strong desire to do the same to them! Had I a frying pan, they'd be laid out like dead fish!!! It may be that to forgive is the dictum in the church in which I grew up, but I have come to believe in the Eastern doctrine of "karma" - you get back what you give out! Granted, I have no desire to inflict pain for my own pleasure, or even view cruelty to any living thing, but I do have a Welsh temper - we're very good at holding a grudge!

I am going to the telegraph office shortly, to see if there is a wire from Vin. I shall be sure to ask Mary if there is anything I can get for her as I know she will not leave her Coop for any reason, now that he is safe and with her again! I would feel exactly the same, were it my Vin who had endured what Coop has! Perhaps she might like me to find some arnica for her bruised cheek - as a matter of fact, I think I shall get some, even if she does not feel the need; I have found it quite uncomfortable to sit since my collision with the inebriated bank teller, and the long ride has not eased the discomfort! I shall also seek out a cafe or restaurant and bring back something for all three of us - the doctor did say that Coop should have soft food or soup until his poor battered mouth heals a bit. This hotel is small, but clean - unfortunately it does not have a dining room, so the hunt for sustenance requires a walk about the town.

COOP

There were voices… but this time they were women's voices… and familiar… Mary… my Mary…

Managin' to crack open my right eye I saw her… she looked so concerned… so beautiful… I *knew* I'd heard her voice earlier… I *knew it*… everythin's gonna be alright now… the bed's so soft… and Mary's nice and warm… and here… warmth… I'm finally warm… it's gonna be alright...

VIN

"And just what evidence have you got that will justify going after Freeman?" The marshal asked as I stood in his office.

"I got eyewitness testimony from two men – one's my cousin and the other is a Pinkerton agent who's also workin' undercover with Freeman," I said, doin' my best to keep my temper in check. It usually takes a lot to get me riled, but worryin' about Coop and the girls ain't done my temper any good. "I just came from Brackettsville, Marshal – my cousin is laid up, hurt real bad from bein' beat to a pulp…. he'll make it, but he and my other agent are both in danger and I ain't got time to argue over this!"

"Hold on, Harper," the marshal said, getting' a bit riled himself, "I believe you, but you're asking me to round up a big posse to go after these fellas and I have to be sure the reasons and evidence are clear as daylight! Freeman's a powerful man and without clear evidence, he could make real trouble for me and my men!"

Hard as it was to stay even-tempered, I managed to say, calm as I could, "You'll have your evidence, Marshal – you got my word on it. How long will it take you to get this posse rounded up?"

He frowned and rubbed his chin, sayin', "Two days – I'm going to need the two deputy marshals as well as volunteers, and they're due back tomorrow – prisoner escort duty. "

"You sure o' that?" I asked, "Every day we delay puts my man in a bigger fix…"

"Freeman's got plenty of good gun hands working for him, Harper," the marshal said, "If you're that worried about your man, get him outta there …."

"All right," I said, lettin' him know by my tone o' voice that I wasn't right pleased with his wafflin' around, "Means I'll need those two days to get to him and get him out, but once he's out, I expect you and your posse to be ready to move, got it?"

"We'll be ready," he said curtly, "Just get a move on and leave the rest to me!"

By the time I got back to my room I was about ready to drop, but I'd promised I'd take care o' lettin' the Widow King know the girls had left, so getting' any rest wasn't in the cards for a while.

"A family emergency?" Mrs. King looked real concerned – she's a nice lady and I didn't really like lyin' to her, but it had to be done.

"Yes, ma'am," I said, lookin' as solemn as I could, "There's sickness in the family and they're needed back in Laramie. I'm here to let you know and pay their board…"

She nodded, still lookin' concerned, and said, "It's not much… they're paid up, all but yesterday and today, so that's all right. Do you want me to pack up their things and send them on to Laramie?"

"That would be real kind of you, ma'am!" I said, relieved that was one more thing I could get off my mind. "Just send it on to General Delivery, iffen you don't mind."

"Not at all," she said, smilin' and pattin' my hand, "Such dear girls – I'm sorry to lose them as boarders!"

"I know they'll be right grateful, ma'am," I said, "I may be movin' on myself soon…not real sure just when, but I'll make sure to get my tally all paid up afore I do."

She smiled at me, her eyes twinkling, and said, "Are you headed to Laramie, too?"

I laughed, and said, "Might just take a look in there, ma'am.. you never know…."

She laughed, sayin', "They really are sweet young ladies, Mr. Vincent - both of them!"

I made my way out to the message drop off, hopin' to get word to

Randall as soon as possible. I knew I needed sleep and wouldn't be much good for anythin' if I didn't get some pretty soon. I'd tied my horse and was just writin' a note when I heard a horseman comin' along the trail... I'd my hand on my gun, but didn't need it, 'cause here came Randall, ridin' right on up! 'Bout time, I thought, I'm due for some luck right about now!

"Howdy, mister," he said, grinnin' at me.

"Howdy yourself," I said, grinnin' back, "Light and set - we got things to talk about!"

The Journal of Jessie Llewellyn Harper

There was a telegram from Vin! He has informed the marshal, but it will take some time before he (the marshal) can get here to Brackettsville - from Vin's rather brief and cryptic wire, I gathered that they are going to make sure that Freeman and his gang are rounded up before coming to interview Coop. I am pleased... and disappointed - naturally, I want my Vin back with me as soon as humanly possible, but Coop needs some time to recover and get back some strength before he is ready to make a statement or testify in court. No one but Vin and the marshal knows exactly where we are -a very comforting thought - and I was able to purchase two or three changes of clothing for me, Mary, and Coop at the general store without too much attention being paid me. I returned to our room with a covered milk pail filled with soup, some coffee, and bread, cheese, and cold beef - not very elegant but filling.

MARY

Jessie went to run some errands and bring back some food for us. Bless her, I know not what we'd do without her! She is our own personal angel as far as I am concerned. She is more than family, she is my chosen sister!

My reverie ended as I realized my Coop had opened his eyes. Those beautiful azure eyes. Or perhaps I should say, eye… Poor baby has such swelling still, that he could only open his right eye.

I tried to smile.

"Do I look that bad, darlin'?" he managed to get out.

I had to swallow hard not to burst into tears! "You look handsome, my dearest."

"I thought you said… you'd… never… lie… to me!" with that he managed a laugh which turned into a cough.

"Here, have some water," I said as I tried to get an arm around him and lift a bit. My darling tried to help but was so weak...

He managed a few small sips, knowing that would be better than gulping… and then sank back against the pillows. He reached towards my cheek but had to let his hand drop back to his side.   "What happened there?... Did you get hurt freein' me?... I'll make the man pay... whoever… hurt you…"

"It's alright, love," I said placatingly, "it was just an accident. Nothing to be concerned with."

Looking concerned but accepting my statement, he asked about Vin. I filled him in as to all that had transpired.

We both looked up as Jessie entered, carrying a pail and a tray filled with breakfast and more importantly, coffee!

COOP

I woke up revelin' in the feel of the soft bed beneath my tired and bruised body… if this was a dream, it was a nice one... openin' my eyes to the feel of a soft hand on my brow, I tried to smile… there was an angel lookin' down at me… my beautiful, brave, sweet gal… Lookin' at her, I remembered that she had risked her own life to free me… it humbled me to think she'd risk such danger to rescue me! That ain't how it's supposed to work… I'm supposed to protect her!

And then there was Jessie, too! Seems like, if one was in need, the other was right there with her… The two of 'em were surely a force to be reckoned with…

Noticin' that I was awake, she brought a cup to my lips. Mmm, that water sure tasted good… maybe I could close my eyes for a little longer… there's someone at the door… just Jessie… and food… and coffee… maybe I *was* in Heaven...

The Journal of Jessie Llewellyn Harper

Mary was pleased that Coop would have some time to recover – being able to care for him was a great antidote to the anxiety and terror with which she has been living over the past weeks! The arnica has helped some, and I can now sit with less discomfort, but I am glad that I do not have to ride for at least a few days!

Coop has told us a little about the gang; not much about his ordeal except some choice Spanish epithets (at least I believe they are epithets - I *must* learn that language!!) directed at his captors. We have reassured him that they will very shortly be in the hands of the law, thanks to him, and he seems more pleased than not, but he is still quite weak and drops off to sleep frequently. Mary does not leave his side - she often touches his cheek, or smooths back his hair, as a reassurance, I believe, that he is really here and alive. It seems to soothe Coop as well, when he sometimes winces or makes a soft painful sound in his sleep.

Thank God, the doctor has reassured us that he will recover well - seeing one you love in such straits is most heart-rending! I cannot share Mary's pain, but just thinking about how I would feel if it were Vin, I can imagine it quite clearly! If there is anything I can do for either of them, I will do it - they are my family now, sister and brother, and so very dear to me!

MARY

I am glad that I let Jessie slather the arnica on Coop's and my bruises. It really has been helping. My beloved can now open both eyes! And it doesn't seem to hurt so much when he smiles, which is what attracted me to him in the first place! His smile that lit up those gorgeous blue eyes… odd how the purple of the bruises made the blue of his eyes 'pop' even more… what a silly thought… it must surely be a result of our recent trials...

Was it just this past spring that my life changed so? So much has happened in so little time! This time last year, I never would have believed my life would have turned out the way it has! Here I was living in the 'wild' West, with a 'real' cowboy… running to the rescue of this man who is the love of my life… and I have a best friend and sister who is worth her weight in gold… and a brother who would fight to the death for us all!

"Whatcha smilin' about, darlin'?"

I turned to look at this beautiful (yes, that's the word, beautiful) man, who loves me, my heart so full I felt it could burst! Following the excitement and uncertainty of the past couple weeks, I began to feel the tears welling in my eyes and I turned away.

He must be getting considerably better, as he clamped his hand down on my wrist. "Darlin'." He pushed himself to a sitting position, with only a little discomfort showing on his features, and pulled me into his embrace. Caressing my back, comforting me, he said, "It's alright, darlin'. It's alright."

Wrapped in his arms, my head on his chest, I could contain the tears no longer. Listening to his voice crooning soothing words and feeling his hands caressing my shoulders, I sobbed, a sense of healing seeping into my very bones. My love was alive, and all would be well. We could relax and heal now…

The Journal of Jessie Llewellyn Harper

It has been six days of waiting and caring for a now almost recovered Coop. The bruises and contusions are beginning to fade, and Coop's strength is coming back, especially now that he can eat "man food" again (his term, not mine!). I know he was getting very tired of soft porridge and soup, poor dear, but one sign of increased health is the strength to complain vociferously! I plan to visit the telegraph office this morning as well as do a little shopping.

VIN

"How are you goin' to handle this, Marshal?" I said as Randall and I stood outside the marshal's office, waitin' for the deputies and the posse.

"Depends on what your man Randall here can tell me," he said, noddin' at Mike.

"Most of Freeman's hands who are involved in the rustling are camped out near Sommer's Creek," Randall said, "I slipped out and far as I know, they're all still there. Freeman was due to come to the camp today with the plans for another big raid. From what I heard, he's got his eye on a trail herd bein' rounded up in the next county and he and his boys are goin' to raid it tomorrow. If we get a move on, we can catch all of 'em today."

"Right," I said, frownin', "Randall knows the camp better 'n me, so he's the likeliest to lead you all in."

Just then, the deputies and the rest o' the posse came ridin' in and the Marshal called his two over to tell them what we were plannin'.

"I know a back trail that'll get us right up to the camp unseen, Harper," Randall said, "You stay to the rear of the posse – that way we got no 'strays' deciding that they'd rather go on home!"

I laughed and agreed. Sometimes men who ain't used to a big fight get cold feet real easy, but Freeman's bunch wouldn't go quiet-like, for sure.

We'd got close to the camp when Randall called a halt. None o' the posse members had shown any signs of wantin' to turn tail, so I rode up front to find out what was goin' on.

"The biggest building in the camp is the cookhouse and bunkhouse – that's where Freeman will be, with most of his men,"

Randall said. "I'll go in first and see if he's there – when I come out, I'll take off my hat if he's in there and you all can come on down... if he ain't, just hold here 'til I can get back with a report – all right?"

We nodded and he rode down around the trees to the camp.

"Sure hope the rats are all in one trap," the marshal said, "I want to get this done!"

"You and me both!" I said, grinnin' at him, "My wife's waitin' for me in Bracketsville and I'm kinda anxious to see her!"

He laughed and said, "We'll try to make sure you get home in one piece, Harper – just make sure the rest of us do, too!"

"You bet!" I said, checkin' that both my handgun and my rifle were ready to go, "I'm guessin' we'll do fine – just hopin' we can get it done as quick and clean as possible!"

One o' the deputies was below the trees, watchin' the camp, and pretty soon he came runnin' up, sayin', "Randall came out and gave the signal, Marshal!"

We rode down, single file, not much above a walk – mostly we all hoped we could surround the bunkhouse and call them outside. Didn't quite work out that way, though....

We'd got almost down to the bunkhouse when there was a shout from inside it. Randall took off, runnin' toward the trees and somebody inside the bunkhouse started shootin'... pretty soon it was firin' and dodgin' everywhere... the boys inside the bunkhouse had cover and didn't want to give up so it looked like a long haul...

I'd got myself behind a shed and was tryin' to see how spread out we all were when I saw Randall slippin' up on the blank wall o' the bunkhouse to the left of the door. Danged if he didn't have a stick o' dynamite in his hands!

I'd no notion he'd carried any and I was about to take better cover when I heard him shout, "Freeman! You and your boys are about to get blown sky high! Throw out your guns or I'll heave this dynamite right in your laps!"

It went real quiet all of a sudden… our men had stopped firin' an so had the crew inside the bunkhouse.

"You're a liar!" I heard from inside - it was Freeman.

"Try me!" Randall shouted and there was a real tense silence all around…….

I shouted out toward the bunkhouse, "Freeman! He ain't lyin'! Unless you and your boys want to get blown to hell in a hurry, throw those guns out… NOW!"

I was close enough to the bunkhouse to hear some arguin' goin' on inside and then another voice, not Freeman this time, hollered out, "OK OK! We give up!"

The door to the building opened just wide enough for us to see a man's arm, throwin' out guns…. I made my way down to Randall, and the marshal and his deputies followed.

"Freeman!" the marshal said loudly, "Get out here – you and all the rest – with your hands up!"

For a couple of minutes I thought we'd have to chance chargin' in, but they came out, one at a time, hands high… Freeman last of all, scowlin' like a thunderstorm, but with his hands above his shoulders. He saw me standin' there and kinda startled like, he said, "Vincent!!

What in hell??"

"Yeah," I said, starin' at him, "and you're damned lucky I'm a Pinkerton man, else I'd take you apart, piece by piece, for what you had done to my cousin!"

"Cousin?" he said, lookin' confused, but still mad as fire, "What cousin?"

"Bobby Fullerton - the man you had your men beat almost to death," I said, feelin' my hand on my gun tensin' with the desire I had to shoot the scum where he stood. "He'll live, no thanks to you, and testify against you at your trial. You're damned lucky he will, else you'd be facin' a rope… and I'd likely be the one askin' to tie the knot!"

All the way back to town with those yahoos all I could think of was getting' a wire off to my Jessie, lettin' her know I'd be there soon as I could. Once we'd got the jail and the marshal's office filled up with rustlers, Randall said he'd stay and see that all the court papers and such got filed. I was right grateful – made sure I put a bit in my telegram lettin' my little girl know to get a room for herself afore I got there! Much as I like Mary and Coop, I wanted my Jessie all to myself – been too danged long since we'd had some time alone!!

COOP

Sure am gettin' tired of not bein' able to do much more than lay here and sleep! I'm afraid all I seem to be doin' is complainin'… I can see a pained look in Mary's eyes… she's been so concerned over me… I know she's worn out… and I lay around mopin'… don't have no right to, after what my Mary and Jessie went through to rescue me!

It still amazes me... watchin' my Mary nappin' beside me... so small and dainty and proper, yet so strong and fierce... reminds me of a story I once read about warrior women called Amazons... hunh... still wonderin' if that story the girls told me about takin' out the guard with a fryin' pan was real... thought I'd dreamt it. Gotta remember to keep on my best behavior anytime I'm in our kitchen back home!

The Journal of Jessie Llewellyn Harper

Vin is on his way to us! The marshal has succeeded in rounding up the miscreants and my beloved plans to be here late tonight! How joyful it will be for the four of us to be together and, God willing, soon on our way home!

Vin, bless him, suggested in his wire that I get my own room – a suggestion I am happy to follow! I arranged it with the desk clerk and will have one of the maids help me move my things... not that I have all that much to move! I did manage to refresh our wardrobes just a bit, thanks to the general store, but we are traveling light for the moment.... fortunately, there was a lovely lawn nightdress just my size at the general store.......

VIN

I got to the hotel after midnight, and the night clerk was kinda reluctant to give me a key to my Jessie's room... poor fella, he turned the color o' spoilt milk when I showed him my gun – and, o' course, my Pinkerton badge! He almost dropped the key into the spittoon by the front desk, tryin' to hand it to me as fast as he could! When I got upstairs, there was a line of light under the door of my little girl's room, so I turned the key and eased in… danged if she wasn't pointin' a pistol at me!

"Oh, my heart!" she gasped, dropping the gun – it was cocked, danged lucky it didn't go off! Before I could say hello, she was in my arms, holdin' on so tight…. not to say I wasn't holdin' her just as close… felt so damned good to have her in my arms again……

The Journal of Jessie Llewellyn Harper

It seems almost impossible that we are so close to Christmas day… I had hoped to be in our own sweet home, decorating a tree cut from our own hills and making all the Christmas goodies with Mary… it is not to be, at least this year. I should not repine though….we are all here, together, and our dearest Coop is mending fast… we have so very much to be thankful for, and this season is about light returning to the world…Vin is sound asleep and I sit here with my Journal, watching him … it seems so foolish to think of gifts and Christmas trimmings when we all have come so close to great loss…

VIN

I woke up slow… felt so good to be done with this job and have my little girl all to myself… she was sittin' at the little desk in our room, writin' in her journal…

I musta made a sound or somethin', 'cause she looked over at me and smiled, sayin', "Good morning, love… you look well rested."

I couldn't help laughin', since "rest" didn't exactly fit what we'd been doin' last night. She gave that little gurglin' laugh o' hers and I patted the bed next to me, sayin', "Rested and ready for anything, little girl!"

She curled up beside me and whispered in my ear, "Te amo, mi corazon…."

Once we'd both finally got up and dressed, Jessie said, "Let's go and collect some breakfast, love, for us and for Mary and Coop!"

"Great idea!" I said, makin' sure I had my wallet tucked in my jacket pocket, "Anythin' else you need, little girl? You and Mary will have to wait 'til we get home to get your things – the Widow is shippin' them to Laramie for ya."

"Not at the moment," she said, puttin' on her hat, "but I do want to find some little things for all of us for Christmas – I do so wish we could all be home to celebrate the holiday, but that will have to wait for next year! At least, we all will be together and that's enough for me, as long as I can find a little something to give us a holiday spirit!"

"Put a ribbon and a bow on yourself, chiquita" I said, grinnin' at her, "That's all I need for Christmas!"

She giggled and tilted her head sideways, considerin' like….. "Just a ribbon and bow?" she said, that little gurgle in her voice.

The picture in my head of my girl dressed in nothin' but a ribbon and bow nearly took my breath away, but I managed to say, even though it was kinda breathless, "That's my kind of Christmas present, chica!"

"Come along, you dreadful man," she said, still gigglin', "Put your mind on breakfast for now – we'll think about Christmas presents later!"

MARY

Vin has joined us. Jessie is so thrilled! Coop and I were just as delighted to see their happiness at their reunion. It was a surprise this morning when there was a knock on our door. We hadn't expected Vin until later today or possibly even tomorrow, yet there he was, standing with a radiant Jessie, holding a tray filled with breakfast treats and a pot of coffee from the cafe across the street!

Glancing over towards my Coop, Vin drawled, "You healed up enough for bacon and eggs yet?"

"You better believe it," replied Coop enthusiastically. "Got the go ahead from the doc two days ago!"

Taking a seat near Coop, Vin sobered and asked, "You sure you're doin' alright?"

"Yeah… How could I not when I have the best nurses in town," laughed my husband, as he nodded towards Jessie and me.

Sitting on the bed next to Coop, I was surprised when Vin reached over and took my hand in his. "Am I forgiven?"

After a pause, I felt my sister's hand rest gently on my shoulder. Looking from her to Vin, I replied, "Of course…" Then I couldn't help adding, "Just don't let it happen again!"

"Yes, ma'am!"

It was after we finished eating that there was a knock on the door. Jessie rose and opened it.

"Excuse me, ma'am. I'm looking for Coop Martin."

"Over here," Vin greeted him.

Coop's eyes widened in recognition. The man laughed when Coop admitted that he thought of him as 'the nice guard' because he always brought food and water and he never hit him!

Vin introduced him as "Mike Randall."

"I wanted to drop by and see how you were doing," Mr. Randall said. "You weren't looking too good the last time I saw you!"

"Thanks to my wife and Jessie, I think I'm gonna live," he replied.

"Yeah, sorry about that… it sure was a big surprise when I went to spring you and found the guard was there on the floor! I thought maybe Vin had come and freed you. It was as I was heading back to the main camp so no one would suspect me helping to free you, when I noticed Vin's horse and then Vin hiding behind some bushes! I thought maybe you weren't hurt near as bad as it looked, and you managed to brain Jenkins with that frying pan and get away all by yourself…"

"Ha! Imagine my surprise when you snuck up behind me," said Vin. "I thought it was you, Mike, who had sprung him! Guess I should've known our girls couldn't be stopped from claimin' all the glory and rescuin' him on their own!"

"Well, I'm just thankful someone finally did! I was gettin' mighty tired of that place," said my Coop. "Not my idea of fun bein' beatin' to a pulp."

Between Vin and Mike Randall and Coop's testimony, it looked like everything would be tied up neatly in no time! It was a relief to discover that the agent was safe and sound as well as our boys.

COOP'S INTERVIEW

"James Cooper Martin, this is Agent Tom O'Reilly with the Pinkerton's," Vin said by way of introduction. He then thumped me on the back and left.

"Mr. Martin," O'Reilly welcomed me, shakin' hands, "This is Miss Tyler, she will be taking notes during the interview." O'Reilly indicated a pretty young lady with brown hair that she had pulled back into a bun, glasses perched on her nose, sittin' at a desk just to the right of the agents' own.

Wavin' in the direction of a chair, he invited, "Won't you please take a seat? I realize you have been through a lot on behalf of our company, and promise this interview will not take long, but it will go a long way in prosecuting the felons." Taking his own chair, Agent O'Reilly began, "Now, Mr. Martin, please describe in your own words the events in which you were involved in this 'Freeman Cattle Rustling' case."

"Where'd you like me to begin?"

"From your first involvement, if you would."

"Well, my cousin, uh, Agent Harper, asked if I'd like to join in on the assignment as I might be able to help…."

After about twenty minutes, we paused briefly for coffee to be brought in as my throat was gettin' mighty dry from all the talkin'.

When I returned to my story, I mentioned how, "There was this one guy, Tyrone, who swore he knew me, and I was usin' a different name… He had been tossed off the wagon train I work for a few years back but fortunately, he never really remembered the circumstances…

I guess he finally convinced them I was the spy though. I think they only kept me alive hopin' I'd give up my partner. They were mighty persuasive but there was no way I'd give up my cousin or the undercover agent! Of course, I didn't know who he was..."

"So that's when you were incarcerated and beaten?" Agent O'Reilly prodded...

"Yes, sir, almost daily and sometimes several times a day."

"Then what happened?"

"I was rescued by my wife and her best friend..."

Miss Tyler's head came up at this. "Your wife?"

"And her best friend, Jessie. Agent Harper's wife."

A small smile played across Agent O'Reilly's lips, "Go on."

"Well, they said they'd found out in town-"

"They were in town?" asked the lovely Miss Tyler.

"Uh, yes, ma'am, you see, when they found out I went missin', they caught the stage from Laramie and headed for Winston." Miss Tyler raised her right eyebrow for me to continue. "And they got jobs in town and found out Freeman was gonna kill me as I 'knew too much,' and since they couldn't find Vin, uh, Agent Harper, they decided to rescue me all on their own."

At this point, we had to pause a few minutes as Miss Tyler had been listenin' instead of takin' her notes, so intrigued was she by the actions of the ladies!

"And just how did they accomplish your rescue?" asked Agent O'Reilly.

"All I know is, I was in a pretty bad way…. I heard whispered voices and there they were, all dressed in black, a gun to the guard's back. He said somethin' that my wife took particular offense to and she decked him with a fryin' pan. I kinda remember that, although not much else."

Over at the smaller desk, Miss Tyler was writin' away, shakin' her head and mutterin', "...a frying pan... incredible... good for her!"

MARY

While Coop and Vin were off at the Pinkerton office for Coop's deposition, Jessie and I went for tea at a local shop near the hotel where we were staying. As we sat there, it began to dawn on me that there were a few small decorations around the place- mainly greenery… some evergreen boughs and such. About then, I realized that Jessie had mentioned something about picking up some gifts for the Christmas celebration in a few days.

I am certain I looked totally baffled… when did Christmas get so close, I wondered… Time passed so very quickly since we left Laramie a few weeks ago to find out what happened to my Coop… How did this happen? This was supposed to be our first Christmas in our new home… a joyous occasion with family and friends… Well, at least we would have the family part right.

My mind came back to the present when Jessie reached over and touched my hand. "Christmas snuck up on me as well! This is the first time you have really been out since Coop recovered, isn't it?"

"It is," I smiled at my sister. "What is today's date?"

"It's the twenty-second. Still enough time to acquire a few items for our husbands for Christmas day!"

COOP

I can't believe I was gettin' tired after doin' so little today. Just that little ol' deposition and I felt done in... Dadgum, but I hate this feelin'!

"What do ya say we stop for a sandwich and a beer?" Vin asked.

Although I could almost hear that bed in the hotel callin' to me, the whole thing was decided when my stomach gave a huge growl, speakin' up for itself!

Vin laughed, "I guess it's settled then!"

Stoppin' in the saloon across from the hotel, we grabbed a couple sandwiches each, and I enjoyed the best beer I ever had in my whole life. Might be because it looked like I wouldn't get a chance to ever have one again just a couple weeks ago... no beer, no food, no sweet Mary... makes a man think about his life some when he almost loses it.

"So, what are you gettin' Mary for Christmas?"

"Had my eye on a pretty ring back in Laramie. Why?"

"Well, it's in three days..."

"*Three days?*" How in hell did that happen? "We ain't leavin' here before then, are we?"

At Vin's shake of the head, I said, "I hafta find somethin' for her. I can't let her think I forgot our first Christmas together!"

"Do you feel up to doin' a little shoppin' before goin' back to the hotel?"

Just the thought made me feel even more tired than I was. "Not really, but I hafta!"

"I could pick somethin' up for you if you want to head on back," Vin said thoughtfully.

"Ha. My wife saves my life and I can't summon enough energy to get her a present? Don't think that'll happen!"

"Then let's get on our mission, so you can catch a nap!"

VIN:

I feel bad for my cousin – he's worn down to a thread… our little "shoppin' trip" was almost too much for him. I was wrackin' my brain to think of somethin' for my little girl when we passed a dress shop. In the front window was a real pretty dress – it was blue, with velvet trimmin's and lace.

I stopped to look closer and Coop bumped right into me, sayin', "Warn a fella, cousin, when you're gonna stop like that! I'd like to get back to Mary less beat up, instead o' more, iffen you don't mind!"

I had to laugh – tired as he was, he still had his sense o' humor! "Just hold on a minute," I said, steadyin' him on the boards of the sidewalk, "Take a look at this, Coop -do ya think Jessie would like it?"

He stared at the dress, turnin' his head this way and that, 'til I was about ready to knock him over, just to get him to give me an opinion!

"Well," he said, kinda slow, "your lady does look real pretty in blue…" He looked sideways at me, grinnin', "Iffen I didn't have my Mary, she'd sure catch my eye in somethin' like this!"

I punched him just a little, on the arm, and he acted like one o' those fellas in a melodrama, groanin' and staggerin' – dang fool! I could feel my face gettin' hot and it was only knowin' he wasn't in the best o' shape that kept me from punchin' him harder!

Once he got done with his little "performance," Coop looked at me and said, "You get her that dress, cousin, and I'll guarantee she'll light right up! She's a fine girl, your Jessie, and gettin' her somethin' pretty is how to show her you think so, too!"

I grinned, and we both went in the shop, kinda startlin' the girl there 'cause we were both laughin' like kids! I hope my little girl likes it – iffen it don't fit, the dress shop girl said they could alter it for her, but not knowin' how much longer we'd be in town, I said, "Tell me, miss, would that one fit you?"

She smiled and said, "Yes, sir, it fits me just about perfectly."

Coop was standin' back a ways, chucklin', as I asked the girl to step out into the shop so's I could see if my guess that she was about my Jessie's size was right. She was real nice about it and just laughed at Coop. I decided that I'd have to take it on faith that she and Jessie were of a size.

We'd got the dress, all wrapped up pretty with ribbons and a bow, and were headed back to the hotel when Coop started laughin' like a danged hyena.

"What's so damned funny?" I asked him. I was still a little embarrassed about shoppin' in a ladies' dress shop, so I guess I sounded more mad than I planned.

"Relax, cousin," Coop said, soberin' up just a bit, "I was just thinkin' about you askin' that girl to let you hug her so's you could be sure she and Jessie were the same size... and imaginin' just what she'd say!"

I grinned, 'cause I'd been thinkin' of askin' just that, but I wasn't gonna tell Coop that!

The Journal of Jessie Llewellyn Harper

I thought I was in for trouble when Vin came back to the hotel after his meeting at the Pinkerton office. He had looked rather glum when he left, and I knew the reason why - his wife and her best friend had "stolen his thunder," so to speak, and rescued his cousin before he had a chance to do it himself! I was thinking about how to soothe his wounded sensibilities when he came into the room with a huge grin on his face, grabbed me in his arms and spun me around like a child's top!! When I had been thoroughly kissed and got my breath back enough to speak, I said, "Not that I'm complaining, my heart, but why the exuberance?"

"Little girl, not only am I a star with Pinkerton, I've got a promotion and a two-week paid leave!"

I was flabbergasted, given his gloomy mood when he left, but I just hugged him and said, "Oh, my darling, how wonderful!"

"You bet it is, mi corazon, and you, little girl, are the reason - you and Mary!"

"Sit down, love and tell me all about it!" I exclaimed, agog to hear just how we could be responsible for such good news.

"Well," he said, holding me on his lap, "my boss was so intrigued and amazed at you two and the 'efficient' way you handled gettin' Coop outta there, that he told me I was brilliant to enlist your help! Bein' the modest fella I am, I told him it was all your and Mary's doin', but he insisted on makin' me the instigator and when he started talkin' promotion and leave time, I let him! You don't mind too much, do you, little girl? I mean, it really was you and Mary and if I'd known what you were up to, I'd a tried to stop you!"

"Of course not, my heart! I'm more than happy to give all credit to you with the Agency! I have no ambitions to be an agent, but I want my wonderful husband to succeed at anything he does. Anyway, when we tried to find you, you were already on your way to get Coop freed - we just happened to overhear some information you didn't have!"

"Thanks, honey," he said, kissing me, "no matter what trouble you get into without me, I'd rather have you than any promotion so, don't get any ideas about helpin' me when I don't know what you're gettin' yourself into!"

This was followed by a would-be stern glare, but he began to laugh and spoiled the effect "Wait 'til I tell Mary that she helped me get a promotion by whackin' somebody with a fryin' pan!"

COOP

Mary was still out with Jessie when I returned to our hotel room. Wantin' to surprise my wife, I hid her gift under my bag in the bottom of the wardrobe. Vin was determined to take us out for dinner tonight to celebrate the completion of the rustlin' case. Lettin' loose of a huge yawn, I decided to try and catch that nap until my gal came back.

Journal of Jessie Llewellyn Harper:

I'd found a lovely shawl for Mary – it was silk with a pattern of green and gold birds – and a silk neckerchief for Coop. I wanted something special for my Vin, but nothing I saw seemed "special" enough! I thought about a pocket watch, but none that I saw was splendid enough for my beloved – all were of tin and rather badly scratched - likely taken in trade for outfitting some poor cowboy who'd needed "grub' for the trail.

I was almost in despair of finding anything at all for him as a Christmas gift, when I caught a glimpse of a leather case high on a shelf in the general store. I'd told Vin that I wished to do my shopping alone and the knowing smile he gave me was even more incentive for finding him just the right thing.

"What is that case, Mr. Stoddard?" I asked the proprietor of the store.

"Don't rightly remember, ma'am," he said, looking up at the shelf, "been there quite a while – my wife took it in trade from a gent about a year ago, as I recall, but she got sick and died real soon after and I guess I forgot all about it. Hang on, ma'am, I'll fetch my ladder from the back and get it down for ya!"

He ambled into the back room and slowly returned with a small stepladder, taking great care in positioning it just so, and then climbing shakily up until he could reach the case. For a moment I thought my request would be the death of him, poor man! He was rather elderly and not very spry, and I had visions of having to run for the doctor after he'd fallen and broken something other than merchandise!

Finally, he was safe and sound, back on level ground and holding the dusty leather case. "Here ya are, ma'am," he said, "it ain't locked, just got a kinda latch on it...."

I took the case, and carefully used my handkerchief to wipe off as much of the layer of dust as I could before opening it. It was a gentleman's shaving kit – but what a kit! The razor had an ivory handle and looked almost new – there was a wrapped bar of shaving soap – unopened - and a brush with an ivory handle, as well as a small ivory cup... the black plush lining wasn't worn or torn... and strange as it seems, inset into the top cover of the case was the very same symbol as my talisman and my wedding ring!

I must have gasped or looked odd, because the old man reached out to touch my arm, saying, "You all right, ma'am? Somethin' wrong with it?"

"Oh, no, sir," I said, smiling at him reassuringly. "Something is very right with it! How much do you want for it?"

He scratched his head and looked thoughtful, "Well, ma'am," he said, don't seem like I remember what my wife gave in trade...how about $10?"

That was a rather steep price, but I said, "That is just fine!" and gave him the money.

As he wrapped up my purchase, he was shaking his head a little, and when I left, I heard him mutter to himself, "Shoulda asked for $20!"

VIN:

Jessie had a big smile on her face when she got back to our room at the hotel – she had a parcel with her and I was reachin' to take it for her when she shook her head and said, "Oh, no, Mr. Harper – you'll have to wait for the morning for this!"

"Looks like you bought more than ribbons and a bow, little girl!" I said, grinnin' at her.

She giggled and said, "Perhaps – you'll just have to wait and see!"

We'd planned to go out for dinner with Mary and Coop tonight, and I knew she'd got a little somethin' for both of 'em, so I said, "Well, I guess I'm just an impatient fella, mi corazon, 'cause you're gettin' your Christmas tonight!"

She looked real surprised and said, "I'm in no hurry, love – I can wait until morning…"

"Nope," I said, reachin' under the bed and pullin' out the parcel with its ribbons and bow, "this one is a Christmas Eve kinda thing."

She looked at the ribbons and the big bow and she turned bright pink, sayin', "Vin! Is there really anything inside that or are you just planning on the wrappings being my present to you?"

I had to laugh – much as I wished I'd thought of it, I had to tell her the truth. "Open it up, chica, and iffen you don't like what's in it, then your idea about the wrappin's will do just fine for you to give me - long as you're wearin' 'em!"

She kinda tried to look prim, but she was still pink, and her eyes were sparklin' when she unwrapped the package.

"Oh, love!" she said, breathlessly, "It's so lovely! And it's my favorite shade of blue – however did you find it?"

"Been takin' 'shoppin' lessons' from you and Mary, chica," I said, "Put that on, so's you can be sure it'll fit ya… the girl in the shop said it could be altered, but I'm hopin' it's the right size...."

Well, it didn't go on right away 'cause I got a Christmas Eve present myself – the wrappin's looked so good on my little girl that we were a little late for dinner.... but that blue dress fit her just fine!

MARY

"Are you sure this looks alright, Coop?" I asked for the third time, as we headed down the hallway on our way to dinner.

"Darlin', you'd make a gunny sack look good."

"That's not what I asked!"

He chuckled. "You, and the dress, look beautiful." Then he slapped my butt and took my hand, saying, "Now let's get to dinner, Jessie and Vin'll be waitin' for us."

As it turned out, we beat Jessie and Vin to the restaurant. But it wasn't a long wait...

"So, Vin," I began, "why the celebration?"

"I hate to admit this but, because of your and Jessie's involvement in the rustlin' case, I got time off *and* a promotion!"

"No! Congratulations! But with news like that I would think *we* should be the ones treating you and Jessie to dinner."

"Well," Vin said, hesitantly, "it's directly involved with a well-swung fryin' pan..."

COOP

After our we dinner order was taken, Jessie pulled out gifts from a bag.

"These are for you," she said, handin' one to me and the other to Mary. "Go ahead, open them!"

"But it isn't Christmas until tomorrow," my Mary pointed out.

With a twinkle in her eyes Jessie patted Mary's hand and said, "It's close enough."

"Good!" I said and ripped into my present. It was a handsome kerchief in a patterned pale blue silk. "Aw, thank y'all. This will look great with my goin' to town suit!"

All eyes were now on Mary. She looked around and then tore into her package. I couldn't help smilin' when she unwrapped a lovely shawl in green with little yella birds on it.

"Oh, but it's so beautiful! Thank you!"

Then reachin' from under the table she passed gifts to both Jessie and Vin. Vin revealed a case, so he could have an occasional cigar, should the mood strike. "Mmm, I do enjoy a cigar, now and again... thank you."

Jessie's gift was a cameo pin which could also be strung on a chain and worn as a necklace as it had a hidden bale.

"Oh! Thank you both so very much! My mother has one similar to this- although, this one is much prettier and can perform double-duty." Handing it to Vin, she said, "Here, love, would you put it on me?"

Mary spoke then, "I feel so blessed to have this special family of the heart!"

"We do too," Jessie said enthusiastically. "Best sister and brother anyone could ever wish for!"

MARY

It had snowed overnight... again! There was a hush in the room. Opening my eyes to the faint, muted glow of sunlight (if it could be called that), I rolled over and discovered that Coop wasn't there!

An abundance of questions ran through my mind... Where was he? Was he all right? Did something happen? Why didn't he wake me? I knew any of my fears were most likely unfounded, but after the past few weeks I suppose I have turned into a mother hen! Getting dressed, I pondered on this. I knew I would have to loosen up on the reins or I would end up smothering Coop, and I couldn't stand it if he began to resent me...

Perhaps I should go across the hall and knock on Jessie and Vin's door? I hated to bother them... but maybe Coop and Vin were off somewhere together... at least I would know if he was with his cousin... and Jessie could help settle my thoughts...

While I was contemplating what to do, there was the sound of a key in the door and the knob turned.

"Hey, darlin'," Coop drawled. "Thought you might be hungry, so I went to the café to bring you back somethin' to eat," he said, as he placed the tray on the bedside table.

Relieved, I hugged him and kissed him.

"That's some response! Hungry?" he laughed. Kissing me back, he then said, "Merry Christmas, darlin'," and he handed me a small wrapped box he had retrieved from the wardrobe. "Open it, sweetheart." I loved seeing the smile on his lips and the anticipation in his eyes... he so loved surprising me...

In a heartbeat, I felt like a little girl again! The present couldn't be jewelry as it felt far too heavy. It seemed I couldn't rip the paper off fast enough! Then my gift was revealed… it was my very own Derringer! "Oh, Coop! How did you know?"

COOP

When I got back to the room Mary was dressed. She looked so relieved to see me that I thought I might be in for a talkin' to! But she just came over to me and wrapped her arms around me and gave me one of the sweetest kisses I can remember… I couldn't wait to surprise her with the gift I'd found… sure hoped she liked it… it's not what most husbands give their wives for Christmas but then, my gal isn't like most wives!

She tore through the wrappin's like a little girl! Her response was more than I could've hoped for…

"Oh, Coop! How did you know?"

It's funny how she can still make me smile when I surprise her… makes me want to do it all the time…

"Didn't think I'd forget our first Christmas together, did ya?"

Lookin' in my eyes, she touched my cheek, so very softly that I could hardly feel it, like she was afraid of hurtin' me… "After all you've been through, I considered the possibility, and it would have been fine, as long as I have you," she said. "I almost forgot it myself."

Lookin' around the room, I asked, "Almost?"

She giggled and went to the bureau and pulled out a tiny box tied with a green ribbon. "This is for you," she said, placing it in my hand.

It was one of them little boxes like holds jewelry... when I got it opened there was a plain ol' gold ring inside. She reached in and then put the ring on my left ring finger. "You once gave me a ring and asked me to wear it, so no other man would look at me and think I was available... I thought it was time that you had one too."

At first, I felt like a branded calf... until I realized how perfectly it fit, that ring... It felt so... right. Takin' that gal in my arms, I felt as though my heart might just burst...

MARY

The boys were in good spirits as we caught the morning stage to Laramie and home. Jessie was tickled that Vin was given a couple weeks off for a job well completed! It was a full coach as there were two other passengers as well as the four of us. The two ladies sat across from each other allowing us to sit as couples. They didn't say very much, remaining aloof, even though we attempted to include them in conversation.

It began to seem a routine enough trip, but Vin had noticed a shotgun guard up top and had asked if there was something he should know, flashing his Pinkerton identification. The old driver told him that we were carrying $30,000 on board! Vin immediately glanced around, and whenever we stopped to change teams he always waited away from the coach. We had changed horses twice already and had only one more stop to make for fresh horses in an hour, when a sequence of events occurred. First, the stage came to a screeching halt just before disaster could strike, thanks to the quick reactions of our driver! There was a suspicious fallen tree in our path. Vin leapt from the carriage as did the shotgun guard, and moved closer to the cover of the trees, one on either side of the road. Then, when Coop got out and assisted the driver with the removal of the tree, four men rode up brandishing weapons and firing into the air! They ordered us out of the coach and suddenly one of the women shouted, "Look out! There are two men in the trees!" Both of the heifers pulled derringers from jacket and purse and pointed them at the driver and Coop!

At that warning, the bandits wheeled their horses and began shooting in the directions of Vin and the 'shotgun' guard! Jessie and I were so angry at these women that we began to beat them most thoroughly with our purse,s and ended up keeping them in place by straddling them and sitting upon their backs! In the meantime, the driver and Coop had run for cover and were now raining fire upon the robbers from their direction! The sheer pandemonium all took place in a matter of minutes before the would-be robbers threw their hands up and surrendered! Two had injuries, which needed to be tended before we could tie them all up and dump them into the coach and continue on to the next stop.

The Journal of Jessie Llewellyn Harper

I was expecting a pleasant stage ride on the last leg from Fort Collins to Laramie - so much for my expectations! After Mary and I had helped to foil a holdup by using our handbags as bludgeons and sitting on our two female captives, our husbands and the driver had subdued the would-be robbers of the stage!

Once they had disarmed and tied the men responsible, Coop and the shotgun guard herded the four miscreants into the stage, with their now rather battered female accomplices. There wasn't any room for Mary and me in the coach, so Coop assisted us to mount two of the robbers' horses, he and Vin riding the other two and keeping pace with the stage, one on either side. Mary and I followed behind, as we were not dressed precisely for riding and much unseemly display of lower limbs was inevitable! Neither of us were willing to try riding sidesaddle on a regular working saddle!!

Our cavalcade made quite a sight as we pulled into the Raynes Relay Station! Fortunately, Mr. Cooper and Mr. Raynes were at home and offered us ladies the comfort of the ranch house, while they and our men escorted the stage full of criminals on into Laramie! It was quite a homecoming!! I fear that our reputations in Laramie will either be ruined or exalted - at least there was no frying pan involved this time.

COOP

I'm beginnin' to think our gals draw trouble their way. What should've been a sweet, simple coach ride turned into a stage robbery attempt! Things started real cautious-like until the women passengers in the stage called out to the robbers about Vin and the guard bein' hidden out of the way. Dadgum, but I hafta shake my head at the feistiness of our gals… those women had no chance in Hell against them!

The two women on the ground were covered with the beginnin' of bruises by the time we got our wives offa them. Jessie's hat was all askew, managin' to hang on her head by a little pin and Mary's purse was layin' in tatters nearby. I managed to drag her offa the surprised and battered woman just as she was aimin' a clawed hand downwards!

"Aim a gun at my husband, hunh? You'll be thinkin' twice next time, won't you?"

The driver and shotgun guard came and collected the women and their male accomplices and, bindin' them, shoved them into the stage.

I will never figure how they do it, but as soon as the situation was under control and I turned to check on my Mary, she went all female on me, buryin' her head in my chest and clingin' on for dear life, sobbin' and shakin'. Lookin' over at Vin I noticed Jessie had done the same, as he was pattin' her back as the tears flowed… just amazin', our gals.

MARY

Mrs. Raynes made us feel so at home. It was such a pleasure to chat with another lady and share our recent adventures. It didn't hurt that our chatting was done over some of Lilian's famous chocolate cake and fresh hot coffee! Such a delight!

Coop and Vin, as well as their cousin, Jess, and Bill Raynes escorted the coach into Laramie to turn the miscreants into Sheriff Wilson. They thought we might enjoy a break at the Relay Station with Mrs. Raynes and promised to return to us as soon as possible. After spending so much time traveling on those hard, wooden seats, we did not protest in the least! It was a pleasant interlude to relax in the comfort of the Raynes' hospitality.

Speaking of delights, young Skip was there as well, taking in all aspects of our tales, interjecting now and then. "What did they do to Mr. Coop?" "They was cattle rustlers?" "A fryin' pan?" "You hit 'em with your purses? They must be pretty heavy!" "Boy, I sure wish I coulda seen all that happen." "Wow! I guess ya don't always hafta use just a gun, hunh?"

"That's right, Skip!" his mother replied calmly, "Being aware of what is at hand can be very useful. Like Jess says, 'You always want to be sure of your surroundings and keep your eyes open!'"

"Yeah! I guess so!"

The Journal of Jessie Llewellyn Harper

Mary and I had a most enjoyable time with Mrs. Raynes and young Skip - that boy has the curiosity of at least a dozen cats! He was enthralled hearing our adventures and I could see that he had visions of foiling robbers and other villains with anything that came to hand - including frying pans!

After we had spent a most pleasant few hours at the Raynes Ranch being regaled with coffee and delicious chocolate cake, our devoted husbands came to fetch us - bless them, they had hired a carriage, so we rode home in style!

Vin didn't tell me until we were safe at home that he had been creased on the upper arm by one of the fusillade of shots, when the bandits were firing at him and the shotgun guard - I sometimes think that masculine stoicism can be most inconvenient! By the time I had cleaned and bandaged him (over his objections!) - nothing more than a graze and I cleaned it thoroughly - we were both most ready to rest and enjoy each other's company without "alarums and excursions!"

"By rights," Vin said, smiling at me as I tidied up my medicinal supplies, "Pinkerton outta give me a couple more days of leave - just for wear and tear."

"I'll be glad to wire them that you are an invalid, my darling, " I said, with a smile, "who needs plenty of bed rest!"

"Now that's a great idea," he replied, grinning and pulling me toward him, "how about startin' that right now?"

"I'd be delighted," I said.

MARY

There is no place like home! The familiar surroundings, sights, smells even… After the recent adventures we found we were still a bit wound up from the excitement of the day, and yet tired all at the same time! Although he had healed pretty much completely from his trauma, my Coop looked drained following our trip home and all the excitement.

"Why don't you go lie down for a nap. I'll fix you something for dinner."

"I'm fine, darlin'," he said, yawning, as I gave him a gentle shove into the nearest comfortable chair.

Searching for something quick to put together revealed that the pantry was pretty bare. As I went to tell Coop that I was going into town to the cafe for something to eat, I was met with the softest snores… so I decided to run over quickly before he even knew I was gone.

"Mrs. Martin, it's certainly good to see you back in town!" I was greeted by Mimi, the proprietress of our favorite cafe. "My, but we've heard tales here! Are they all true?"

Caught off guard as it had only been a couple hours since our return, I replied, "I suppose that all depends! What have you heard?"

"That you and Mrs. Harper stopped the stage coach from being robbed all by yourselves with nothing but your purses!"

Laughing, I replied, "We did have a little help from our husbands, the driver *and* the 'shotgun' guard!"

Returning home with Coop's dinner, I looked forward to relating the story of our exploits to him, not to mention to Jessie and Vin tomorrow. I suppose this was life in a small town!

Entering the house, I discovered a very agitated Coop! "Where'd you go?" he asked almost frantically.

"Down the street to Mimi's. We didn't have anything, so I thought this would be quickest," I explained calmly, setting the food down on the kitchen table.

"Oh, that makes sense." He ran his fingers through his hair. "I just... couldn't find you..."

It was at this point that I realized that my Coop hadn't recovered completely from his recent trauma quite as much as I thought, as this reaction was very unlike him!

"Come on, dearest, have a seat and some food." I led him to a chair at the table. "The water should be almost hot enough for a nice bath by the time you're finished and then we can go to bed. How does that sound?"

"Like Heaven!" he exclaimed, with that little boy smile of his.

Finishing his meal, he rose and stretched. I was already in the tub as he came in. Rising from the bath, I said, "Here you go. It's still nice and warm."

He stood there appraising me.

Holding out my hand, "Pass me the towel?"

"Must I?"

"If we're to get to bed, yes!"

"I think I'll skip the bath..." he said taking the towel and drying me.

"Well, I think we have fresh sheets on the bed, and someone needs to get the dust off before he climbs under them!"

Hanging his head in mock resignation, "I'm not gonna to win this one, am I?"

"I'm afraid not, dearest!" I replied, as I assisted him to undress.

"That's really not helpin', darlin'!"

"Then finish it yourself. I'll be waiting in the bedroom when you're done," I said with a smile. "And wash your hair with that fancy shampoo I bought in St. Joseph!"

It wasn't even ten minutes later when a still damp Coop joined me....

"Oh, Coop...." My, but it's good to be home!

The Journal of Jessie Llewellyn Harper

Vin and I were reasonably well rested this morning - our activities last night didn't hurt his poor arm in the least as he so ably demonstrated! We decided to drop by Mary and Coop's place to see if they wanted to go to town with us - the carriage needed to be returned to the livery, but we expected to have quite a bit of shopping to do and that could wait until after our purchases had been conveyed back home.

They were pleased to join us, although Coop looked just a bit tired. He was quite cheerful, however, as was Mary - I am sure they celebrated his recovery and our return home last night, as did Vin and I. We went our separate ways - Vin and I to the general store and Mary and Coop to the cafe for lunch.

As I was collecting some of our needed supplies, I heard Vin talking with Mr. Drummond, the storekeeper.

"That's some lady you've got, Mr. Harper!" said Mr. Drummond.

"She is, for sure," Vin responded. "You gonna get her and Mrs. Martin to join the next posse?" said Mr. Drummond, "I hear they're a pair of tough customers!"

Vin chuckled and said, "So what makes you say that, sir?"

"It's all over town how they beat up a couple of no-goods and saved the strongbox on the stage!" Mr. Drummond said, "Hear tell they did it all with just their purses!"

Vin said something I couldn't hear clearly, and Mr. Drummond guffawed.

I had all I needed and walked back to the counter, all the while thinking, "Oh, heavens! Now we're notorious!"

I approached Mr. Drummond, set my purchases down on the counter and reached into my bag for some cash. The silly man pretended to be terrified and shrank back, saying, "Please, Mrs.

Harper, ma'am, don't hurt me!!"

He and Vin began laughing like hyenas, drat them, so I just handed Mr. Drummond my payment and said, as sweetly as a jar of molasses, "I won't, dear sir, unless my husband asks me to!"

Vin looked at me and then said to the storekeeper, "Better be careful, Drummond - she don't always wait to be asked!"

We left the store, to Mr. Drummond's obvious disappointment, and walked over to the cafe to join Mary and Coop - I must admit I was secretly pleased at my new "reputation" as a "tough customer," although I think it was said in jest! Vin regaled Coop and Mary with the story of Mr. Drummond's witticisms and Coop looked at my "sister," grinning like a fool, and said, "Well, darlin', you gonna run for sheriff with Jessie as your deputy?"

She poked him in the ribs, none too gently, and replied, "I just might!"

Our husbands looked at one another and startled the customers in the cafe by their uproarious laughter!

Made in the USA
Columbia, SC
04 December 2019